# BORN FROM A WISH

## DINO JONES

Born From A Wish Copyright © 2020 Dino Jones

All Rights Reserved. No part of this book may be reproduced, scanned or transmitted in any forms, digital, audio or printed, without the expressed written consent of the author.

ISBN 9798682365609

First edition, September 2020

# CONTENTS

**PROLOGUE: A TIME FOR TWO**  3

**PART I: DAYDREAMS AND FORGOTTEN MEMORIES**

1  Daydreamer Albert    18
2  The Red-Haired One    55
3  Beyond The Veil    106

**PART II: DUKE'S END**

4  Albert Flew Over The Cuckoo's Nest    130

**PART III: UNDER THREE PALMS**

5  Homecoming    168
6  The Sexothèque    185
7  Paradise    214

Prologue

# A Time For Two

As he stepped upon the cobblestone street, a growl of thunder in the distance made him turn his head around. *Rain's on the way*, he thought to himself as he continues walking down the busy city street. He doesn't have a particular destination in mind. His feet just kind of move him along. It's late afternoon and the sun hangs low in the sky peeking through the gathering clouds. He approaches a crosswalk and stops at the edge of the curb. The cars passing in front of him create a draft that nearly causes him to lose his favorite cap perched atop his crown. He sighs and firmly adjusts his black baseball cap tighter. There are too many people on the street and he wants to get away from them all. He looks across the street and sees a park that looks nice and quiet. The walk signal mercifully lights up and he makes a break for the parks main gate.

He enters the park and breaths a sigh of relief. "Whew! Finally…God, I hate being me. Feeling this way is the absolute worst," he said as he took a seat upon a wooden park bench. He removed the wire frame glasses from his face and stared at them. "I hate wearing these ugly things," he continues to muse out loud to himself as he slides his glasses into the inner pocket of his bright red jacket. He sits a moment with a grimace upon his face. "I don't wanna be me no more," he said, glumly.

As he looks across the open expanse in front of him something catches his eye. A large fountain shoots crystal clear water into the darkening sky above. He watches, captivated by the falling water, then decides to investigate it closer.

He takes the short walk to the fountain and upon closer inspection sees that countless shimmering coins littered its base. He reaches into his pocket and withdraws a glimmering quarter. It glistened in the warm light of the setting sun as he flicked it into the fountain. Upon meeting the surface of the crystal clear water, it produces a loud 'PLINK!' and settles among the other coins at the fountains base. He closes his eyes and thinks to himself, *I wish to be someone else.*

He slowly opens his eyes and finds himself staring up at the orange hand of the crosswalk signal once again. *What the? Was I daydreaming again?* He stares across the road where the parks gate was and is astounded to see nothing but darkened buildings. *Had the park ever really been there?*

The signal changes and he lets out an audible sigh. He doesn't know what to believe but his feet begin to move him forward once more. He steps forward and bumps into someone. "Excuse me," he said without thinking.

"No, that was my fault," a girl said. He turns to see her smiling at him. She was wearing a pair of mirrored sunglasses and a bright yellow baseball cap with an enamel pin of three neon colored palm trees stuck to it. The palm trees caught his eye and he began to stare. "Has my pin caught your eye?" she asked, still smiling.

He averted his eyes and said, "Oh, yeah…It's neat."

"Thanks," she said, laughing.

He shifts his gaze back to the pin of the three palm trees when the sound of car horns startle him. He looks around to see that the pedestrian signal had changed and they were in the middle of the street holding up the flow of traffic.

"Whoops! Hey, I know this café around here that serves a great cup of tea. Are you interested?" the girl asked. His eyes go wide with surprise and he slowly shakes his head up and down. He's in disbelief that this girl would want to invite him anywhere. "Cool! Let's go," she said as she grabbed his hand. He begins to feel his face grow warm. He's thankful that she's leading the way and facing away from him. He prayed that she wouldn't turn around and look at him. If she were she would see both of his cheeks a rosy red color.

She led him to a small café a few minutes later. It was like something you'd see in a small European town. It looked pretty cozy inside. "Here we are! Now for that tea!"

"Here try this," she said, handing him a ceramic mug adorned with blue spirals. Steam rose from the contents within. He decides to let it cool for a bit. "So, what's your name?" she asks looking at him over her piping hot cup of tea. The steam had slightly fogged her lenses.

"James," he blurts out. "Yeah, James."

"Well, James, try the tea…you're gonna love it. My name is Kate."

He lifts the mug to his mouth and lightly sips on it. "It's…delicious," he said as he began to drink heartily from the mug.

"I told you!" Bright flashes of light illuminate the darkened street outside followed by a torrential rain seconds later.

"Oh, geez. Looks like it's going to be a bit before we can get outta here," James said as he watched sheets of rain begin to pelt the large window of the café.

"That's OK. I love this little café. It's nice and quiet. Sometimes I like to come here and just sit alone and think." The two sit in silence listening to the sound of falling rain upon the roof. It was very relaxing. "Oh, I've got an idea! How about we play the crane game? Maybe you can win me a little something?"

James remembered seeing a lone prize grabber in the back corner of the café when they had walked in. He recalled it being full of multicolored teddy bears. "Sure. I got this."

She lit up like a Christmas tree. "Yeah? Let's do it!"

James approaches the prize grabber and inserts a few quarters into the coin slot. The machine springs to life and begins to play some upbeat music. He sees a cute brown bear sitting right on top of his brethren in the middle of the machine. He eyeballs James with his tiny black eyes. James wraps his hand around the lever and makes his move. He positions the claw above the bear and presses the red button in the middle of the lever. The claw descends upon him and slowly plucks him up. As the bear is being lifted he sways back and forth, slightly squeezing out of the grip of the claw. James holds his breath as the claw continues to move agonizingly slowly towards the prize drop.

It feels like ages have passed when the claw finally releases its grip and the bear falls into the hole below. James exhales loudly in relief. "YAY! You did it, James! Man, that was intense!" He reaches into the machine and pulls out the bear. It has a large smile upon its face. *Had that been there before?* He questions himself. He tries to inspect the bear further but Kate plucks it from his hands. "Thank you, James!" She gives James a quick kiss upon his cheek. This time he lit up like a Christmas tree. "What should his name be?" Kate coos.

James thought for a moment. "How about Tony?"

"Yes! Your name is Tony!" Kate smiled from ear to ear and pressed Tony tightly into her chest.

"Hey, it looks like the rain has let up out there," James said as he turned toward the large window.

"Let's go for a little walk, James. I always enjoy walking after a fresh rain," Kate said, still holding Tony close.

They exit the café and begin to walk side by side through the neon washed alleyways. "Isn't the street so lovely right now, James?" Kate said as she held Tony in her arms. The bright neon-lit signs reflected against Tony's tiny black eyes. He agreed that the pinks and purples reflecting off of the damp street below did produce quite the aesthetic. They turn a corner and discover the beginning of a boardwalk circling the nearby lake. "Oooh, a boardwalk! Sounds romantic. Let's check it out." Before long the two of them find themselves walking alongside a large lake. A light mist hangs in the air and gives the darkened water a bit of an eerie feeling.

"This is nice," James said, leaning against one of the metal railings. He looked out upon the lake and watched as the reflections of the lanterns hung along the edge of the boardwalk, stretched and became distorted by the ripples on the surface of the water.

"What are you thinking about?" Kate whispered as she leaned next to him.

He looked over at her and saw both her and Tony looking up at him. A smile formed across his face and then he began to chuckle. "Nothing much...just enjoying the view." Kate smiled and nestled closer to him. He felt his cheeks begin to warm again.

"Hey, James, you wanna see a place with an even better view?" Kate said, looking up at him.

"Even better than this? Where is it?"

She smiled and took a step back. "It's my secret spot. Come on. I'll show you! It's not too far from here."

The two leave the boardwalk and take off towards Kate's "secret spot". After a bit of a walk down some more alleyways and up an elevator, he finds himself atop a multistory car park. A few vehicles sit parked in the distance on the opposite side of the top floor. "Come on, James. Up here! Hold Tony for a moment," she said as she passed Tony to him and hopped up onto an elevated platform. James passes Tony back to her and then follows her onto the platform.

Once he climbs onto the platform he sees her standing only a few steps from an open air drop. It makes him nervous to see her so close to the edge. "Take a look," she said, standing tall with no fear. He gingerly approaches the edge cautiously and looks out. He stands in awe next to Kate.

This secret spot is perched high above the neon lit city below. He wasn't aware that they had gone so high up in the elevator. He watches in the distance as driven lights move randomly, the never ending show. "Breathtaking isn't it?" she said. He looks over at Kate still wearing her mirrored sunglasses. *You're breathtaking*, he thought to himself. "You ever wonder what it would be like to be someone else?" Kate said, clutching onto Tony tightly. "I think about that sometimes…"

James turns towards her and looks at her. He feels a profound sadness emanating from her. "Why would you ever think such a thing? *You* are breathtaking. " She forces a smile and wraps her arms around him. Tony is in the middle pressed between the two of them.

"You really think so? What's so special about me? I wouldn't say I'm breathtaking."

James looks at her for a second. His reflection stares back at him as he slowly removes her sunglasses. She holds her eyes closed. "Open your eyes, Kate." She slowly opens them and two dark brown eyes stare back at him. They're just as dark and mysterious as Kate herself but they also invoke a feeling of great nostalgia deep within himself.

He removes her baseball cap next. The three palms reflect the neon light below. Fiery red hair catches him by surprise. Her bangs fall over her left eye and move slightly in the breeze. He stands looking at her, completely captivated. How could she think such things? "You're…beautiful. Just beautiful." Tears begin to stream down her face. She hugs him as tight as she can. "You're perfect," he said as he breathed deeply of the scent of her hair. He could swear that he smelled light hints of saltwater.

"So are you." She reaches up and tosses the black cap upon his head over the ledge. He watches as it falls out of sight. She reaches into his jacket and slides her hand into the inner pocket and pulls out his glasses. She places them upon his face and smiles. "There…You don't need to hide away or pretend to be someone else. I love you…Albert."

He looks deeply into her eyes for a few seconds and replies, "…I love you too, Elly." The two tightly embrace one another upon the ledge. Their little bundle huddled between them.

As they continue holding one another, Albert notices a sound growing from the streets below. He tries to ignore it. It's quiet at first, but quickly rises up the side of the car park until it's impossible to ignore.

Elly takes a step back. "I hate goodbyes," she said as fresh tears began to stream down her face. She holds onto Tony and shakes him lightly. "Thank you," she said. "We'll meet again soon, love."

Albert wakes to golden early morning sunlight illuminating his room. His alarm blared in his ear upon his bedside table. He killed the alarm and lay there in the afterglow of his dream. He decided it felt like more than just a simple dream. "Vision" seemed more appropriate. As he lay there he could feel it slipping ever so slightly from his mind. "Alby! Up, up, up! It's time for school!" Albert's mother said from outside of his room.

Albert rolls his eyes. "I'm awake," he said, annoyed.

After Albert showered he joined his mother for breakfast. "Good morning, Alby. Hey, are you excited about Halloween? You and Sydney are going out trick or treating again this year, right?"

"Didn't I tell you? We're supposed to go out to Miracle Pier tonight. I mean I'm 13 now, Ma. I can't go out trick or treating forever."

"Oh, that's right. So, it's just going to be you two hanging out at the amusement park?"

"No, we're meeting up with Victoria there and a friend of hers...but I kind of feel like a third wheel these days since he met Victoria..."

"I'm sure they don't look at you like that...But you said Victoria's bringing a friend? Is this going to be a...double date?"

Albert looked away slightly embarrassed, "I suppose you could call it that."

"That's great! You should take her on the Ferris wheel. It looks out over the lake. It's very romantic."

"…Romantic, huh?" he replied, as he thought back to his romantic walk along the boardwalk with Elly. "I'll keep that in mind, Ma."

"Oh, where's your hat this morning? You always wear your black hat."
Albert smiles. "I tossed it in the trash earlier. I just felt…like I didn't wanna wear it anymore."

"Really? Are you feeling OK?"

"Never better," Albert said, continuing to smile. "I just had this really vivid dream last night. It made me very happy."

"OK, Alby…it's completely normal for you to have those kinds of dreams at this age."
Albert frowned and shook his head, "No, no! Not that kind of dream! A girl was in it though…but it wasn't like that."

"What did she look like?" she asked as a look of concern spread across her face.
"She had fiery red hair."

"I see," she replied as she quickly stood up and walked into the kitchen. "You should be getting ready for school, Albert. Don't forget your vitamin." She came back to the table and handed him a pill. Albert downed it with a big gulp of orange juice.

"Thanks, Ma," Albert said, walking to his room to change out of his pajamas. Another day of middle school lay before him.

Throughout the day, Albert thought of walking through the neon-drenched city streets while holding onto Elly's warm and loving hand. His dream had brought him great happiness but as the day continued he could gradually feel the finer details of the dream slipping away from him. He mostly shrugged it off. He remembered that everyone typically forgot their dreams when they woke up. Something felt a bit off though with him. It was hard to explain but it felt as if something inside of him was becoming dull. He put it out of his mind and held onto as much of his dream as he could.

Elly wasn't far from his mind during his evening out at Miracle Pier. The double date was a disaster on his end. He felt it was nothing but a waste of time. He was only interested in one girl and that was Elly. That night when he drifted off to sleep he prayed to see those dark, mysterious eyes staring into his once more but the only thing that greeted him was the darkness and nothing more.

Elly sat in the café alone. She left Tony at home tucked in bed. The setting sun cast long shadows upon the wall behind her. She sat with her arms crossed on the round table in front of her as she looked outside of the large window as the neon lights of the city outside sprung to life. *Looks like I won't be seeing him tonight,* she thought as she continued to wait and wonder.

# PART I
# DAYDREAMS AND FORGOTTEN MEMORIES

# Chapter 1

# Daydreamer Albert

Blackness. Cold, blackness filled with despair. That's what Albert feels as he stares vacantly at the rugged ceiling above him tucked tightly into his bed. As he lies there he hears the rumbles of passing vehicles driving by outside of his window into the night. "That old familiar feeling again…I'm twenty-one years old now…yet I always end up feeling empty inside like this." Albert muses to himself as tears begin to well up in the corners of his dark brown eyes. "What's the point? I'm never gonna meet 'the one' anyway." Tears begin to stream down Albert's face and pool onto his pillow.

    A few days earlier Albert was on top of the world. Albert stands in the shower lathering up his light brown hair and listening to some music blaring out of his shower radio he had received for Christmas just a few short days prior. Some cheesy 80s love song plays on this local AM station. A song most people might make fun of due to all the clichés within but not Albert. Not today anyway, today he's on cloud nine. Interestingly enough that's the title of the tune. "You make me feel like I'm on cloud nine, baby!" Albert sings, albeit painfully off-key, his little heart out.

Albert finishes up his private concert for one and steps out onto the fluffy blue bath mat outside of the tub. He steps towards the mirror and wipes the steam away and stares at his reflection. "Whoa, who's that handsome guy?" He turns his left hand into a makeshift phone and holds it to his face. "Hello, 911 emergency? There's a handsome guy in my bathroom…wait a second, cancel that. It's only me." He throws his head back and lets out a bellowing laugh at his foolishness.

He looks into the mirror again this time with a serious determined look on his face, "Alright, enough of that. Today's the day we make our move on the lovely librarian. Our Hispanic cutie." A smile spreads across Albert's gleaming face, still moist from his shower.

A knock comes from the opposite side of the door followed by, "Alby, don't use up all the hot water! I wanted to take a bath soon," his mother said followed by silence from Albert. "You hear me in there, Alby? You OK?" She knocks again and begins turning the doorknob. Slight hints of panic in her voice. Images flash in her mind of Albert laid out on the bathroom floor, blood pooling underneath him.

"YES! I heard ya, ma! Please, I'm trying to finish up in here!"

Albert's mother steps away from the door, "Alright, don't be so grouchy," she said and walked away up the hallway leaving Albert alone once more, rolling his eyes.

Albert dries himself from head to toe with his black towel then wraps it around his lower half, opens the door, and darts across the hall to his bedroom. He shuts the door behind him then turns the lock. Tossing the towel aside he stands in the middle of his room naked, contemplating what to wear on this big day.

He walks over to his closet door and opens it up. His wardrobe stares back at him. "What the hell am I gonna wear?" he mutters to himself, hands on his hips. Albert's eyes glance left to right over everything. Albert immediately fixes on his favorite cardigan. It's a black one with lime green bands on the sleeves. A smile spreads across Albert's face, "Yeah, I can wear that with a t-shirt underneath and some jeans. It'll be a dressy kind of laid back look! She's gonna love it!" He quickly grabs his selection off the rack and hastily dresses, all the while humming the tune he was belting out earlier during his "concert".

Finally dressed, he darts back across the hall into the bathroom and stares at his reflection once more, steam still surrounding the edges of the mirror. Albert notices his hair is all over the place and quickly opens the medicine cabinet behind the mirror and retrieves his hairbrush and begins to comb through his fine light brown locks. Albert styles it much the same as he has his entire life. Brushing a side part and separating his hair into two sections. It's a look he's felt comfortable with and never deviates from. After he's fixed his hair to his liking he reaches back into the cabinet and grabs the bottle containing his daily vitamins. He pops one into his mouth followed by some water from the faucet and swallows it down. Albert, always a creature of habit, never deviates from his routine and repeats it each day in this exact order.

Once satisfied with his hair, Albert snaps his finger and gives a wink and a quick point smiling at his reflection. Switching the light off, he walks down the hall into the living room where his mother is sitting down reading through a light romance novel. She looks up at him as he's about to turn the handle of the front door and walk out, "Albert, where are you off to looking all dapper? Did you take your vitamin? Oh, wait a second. Don't you have a date?"

Albert blushes and turns around, "Yes, to both. I'm meeting up with Yvonne this afternoon, remember?"

A toothy grin forms on her mouth, " Oh, yes, that's right! Don't forget that soup you asked me to make for her. I do hope she gets to feeling better. You have fun and be sure to bring her home to meet me soon!"

Albert rolls his eyes at her, "You'll meet her, Ma. Don't worry."

"OK, Albert. You be careful. I love you. Let me get that soup ready."

Albert's mother stands up and walks over into the kitchen and removes a Tupperware container from the fridge containing a delicious homemade chicken soup. She places it into the microwave for a few minutes as Albert paces the floor back and forth creating a bit of a tread in the beige carpet. Finally, the microwave bell issues a loud DING! and before his mother can call out to him to come and retrieve the soup he is already grabbing it from the microwave in a flash. "Wait up, Alby! Come here and let me kiss your head," she said, laying her book down.

Albert stops right as he's about to turn the doorknob to leave. "OK, Ma...," Albert begrudgingly replies, walking over to her. He kneels down and she plants a kiss on the top of his head as she has done every day of his life.

"OK, I'm outta here," Albert quickly said and ran out the front door grasping onto the soup in his hands with his pack on his back. He enters the chilly early January day slamming the door behind him and breathes in a deep breath of the brisk air exhaling a cloud of fog from his nostrils. "It's gonna be quite the year!" Albert says to himself, "1998 is gonna be one of those years I'll never forget. I can just feel it." He continues to muse to himself as he begins to take off up the street heading for the library in uptown Lando.

It's a chilly day in Lando, Alabama. Typical for this time of year, but Albert can still feel the sun's rays on his back warming him as he walks along down the sidewalk lost in thought. Thoughts of Yvonne flood his mind and he can feel the butterflies begin to swirl all about inside of him. It's a feeling he's grown quite accustomed too on the walks down to the library these past few weeks. As he walks along down the sidewalk his mind begins to drift back to that day he first met Yvonne.

Being an avid reader, Albert had been in and out of the library so much that the ladies who ran the place knew him by name. The same group of ladies had run the place for as long as Albert could recall and he liked this sameness. Nothing out of the ordinary ever occurred during his visits. Everything and everyone was always where he left it. This comforted him and made him feel safe and secure.

It was shortly after Thanksgiving though, during one of his routine visits, that the sameness changed. During this visit, nothing was out of the ordinary at first. Things seemed as they had been every other time he visited. Albert walked to the horror section and began pulling books out left and right from the stacks. Some of the selections he made were based solely on the cover art, others based on the blurbs on the back and inner covers. Whittling his selections down to a manageable ten books he brought the books stacked up in two columns of five books each.

"Did you find everything well?" a voice spoke from behind the two stacks. Albert, perplexed by the voice, looks over the books and sees no one. A hand moves between the two stacks and pushes them aside. Staring back at Albert sits a petite raven-haired girl with light brown eyes. Albert quickly averts his eyes looking down upon his black and white sneakers. "Hi, there. Did you find everything well?" The lovely girl repeats. Albert shakes his head up and down his face beginning to grow warm. *Who is this girl? What happened to Dolores?* Albert thought to himself.

"Can I have your library card, sir?" the lovely girl asks. Her soft voice makes Albert blush further. He reaches into his pocket and pulls out his wallet, fumbling it and dropping it onto the floor. The lovely girl giggles softly at Albert's clumsiness, but not in a nasty way he feels. He laughs a bit at himself too. He retrieves his card and with his eyes still averted he hands it to the girl. She reaches out for it and one of her soft warm fingers brushes ever so softly against one of Albert's and he feels drops of sweat begin to develop on his brow.

The girl turned away from Albert and he quickly stole another glance at her. Her skin, a dark brown, is not without imperfections. She has a few pimples on her face but this doesn't bother Albert in the slightest. Albert had a few pimples of his own, mostly scattered about his back. One thing that caught his attention was a beauty mark on the left side of her face beside her mouth. Albert found himself staring at it for a moment longer than he should have and she turned her gaze back to him.

Albert finds himself gazing down upon his old beat-up shoes once more. "OK, Albert, your books will be due back December 14th. Enjoy your reads and have a wonderful day," the lovely girl said cheerfully, a bright smile beaming from her mouth. "Oh, and my name is Yvonne. I look forward to seeing you next time!" Yvonne's bright smile continues to beam as Albert forces his gaze up, locking eyes with her for a brief moment. He forces a smile, the sweat from his forehead stinging his eyes, and quickly makes for the front door.

Albert throws it open and takes a big breath of the cool air outside. His mind is running about a million miles an hour. *Yvonne*, Albert repeats in his mind. He goes over and over that moment her soft finger grazed his. He contemplates everything during his ten-minute walk home from the Lando Community Library or the "LCL" as the locals like to call it for short. In his mind, Albert goes over every detail from the most noticeable, her navy blue LCL t-shirt, to the most minute, the way she lightly tapped what seemed to be a song as she sorted out Albert's books on the computer. When Albert reaches his house he's already fallen in love with her.

Albert gleefully opens the front door and shuts it behind him, locks clicking into place. The living room is filled with the smell of freshly cooked steaks, Albert's favorite. "Albert, supper's ready!" his mother calls out. *This day just keeps getting better and better*, Albert thought to himself as he kicks his shoes off and skips along to the kitchen.

"Hi, ma!" Albert cheerfully said to his mother as she stood in front of the stove flipping a delectable t-bone steak over on the skillet. The smell enveloping the kitchen began to make Albert's mouth water.

"Well, someone's in a good mood it seems. What were you up to, Al?"

Albert begins to blush and looks down at the gray socks on his feet. "Oh, you know...I met someone at the library," he said, a smile spreading across his face.

His mother turns to face him. "You met someone?" she inquires curiously.
"Yep. A girl. Her name's Yvonne. She just started working there. She and I really hit it off. We talked for what seemed like hours and she held my hand."

Albert's mother walks over to him and puts her arms around him. "That's wonderful!" she said, excitedly. "I knew you'd meet someone down there eventually that you connected with!"

"OK, Ma. Geez, calm down," Albert said, lightly pushing her off of himself, chuckling softly.

Albert began to smell the scent of smoke and right on cue, the fire detector began to blare. "Oh, my stars!" his mother yells and takes the slightly burnt steak off of the skillet and places it upon an ornate plate. Albert reaches up and hits the button upon the smoke detector silencing it. "Umm, I'll have this one," Albert's mother said as they both laughed.

The two sit down and begin to eat. She begins to question him on what all he and Yvonne had talked about. Albert eagerly proceeded to fill her in on how the two had walked around for a good hour or more through the library stacks discussing their favorite authors and novels and how Yvonne had embraced him, grabbing his hand and how he felt very happy. Albert's mother was ecstatic to hear all of these details as was Albert to share them.

After supper Albert retreats to his room, his belly full and his mind still brimming with thoughts of Yvonne. He falls upon his bed staring up at the ceiling. His mind wandered and his eyelids grew ever so heavy. Albert drifts off and has the most wonderful dream.

In this dream, he and Yvonne are married and are living together in a wonderfully large palatial estate on the coastline of a tropical island. Albert lies in his king-size bed feeling a warmth beside him. He turns and sees Yvonne fast asleep nestled into his side, a vision of pure beauty. He feels a deep sense of happiness that all's right with the world.

He slowly rises out of the bed careful not to wake her and walks over to a set of doors leading out to the bedroom terrace. Upon the terrace, Albert gazes upon a beautiful sandy beach below peppered with green grass. A rich Hawaiian breeze caresses his cheek softly. His gaze shifts across the bay of crystal clear water, diamonds of light from the setting sun dance upon the waves, to the emerald hills in the distance darkening at each passing moment. Night is falling upon this utopia.

"Hi, love." Albert hears the soft voice of an angel and turns around to see Yvonne cloaked in a beautiful red velvet robe and nothing more. Normally upon seeing such a sight as this Albert would avert his gaze and look down upon his feet, but not here. He looks into her dark brown eyes and is struck with an odd feeling. He felt as if Yvonne weren't herself. It was a completely ridiculous feeling. He shrugs it off and walks up to her and kisses her deeply. She wraps her arms around him softly pulling herself closer to him.

After their passionate embrace, the two gaze upon the splendor of this paradise. He notices one detail he had overlooked earlier. Way off in the distance upon the beach, three palm trees swayed back and forth in the cool island breeze coming off of the bay as the last rays of sunlight fell behind the emerald hills in the distance. A crescent moon shined down upon them. It's here that Albert began to hear a knocking and the two turn around. Albert looks over to Yvonne and at this moment she's no longer Yvonne but a red-haired woman with dark piercing eyes and a sly grin on her porcelain face.

The knocking continues and Albert is jarred from his dream. KNOCK! KNOCK! KNOCK! Albert hears again. He looks at his watch. '10:37' it reads. *It's only been a few hours*, Albert thought to himself as he stands up and walks to his door. He flips the lock and opens his door to find his mother standing outside in the hall. "I just came to check on you, Al. I saw your light was still on but you were being awfully quiet," she said, a look of concern spread out upon her face.

Albert smiles at her, "I'm OK, Ma. I drifted off. You woke me from this wonderful dream I was having."

"Oh, I'm sorry. I was just making sure you were alright. I'll let you get back to bed. Night night, Alby."

He winced a bit and softly said, "Goodnight."

Albert didn't care to be called Alby. It was what he used to be called by her when he was very young. Albert's mom certainly liked babying him but now that he had another woman in his life the time had come to stop such things. He had tried to talk to her about that before but the conversation went in one ear and out of the other.

Albert made his way back over to his bed and crawled into it. Thoughts of that wonderful dream came back to him. He thought of Yvonne's soft form in her velvet robe, clinging to her every curve. He also thought of the red-haired one…the woman he was holding at the end. Albert can't shake the suspicion that he's seen her somewhere before. Her eyes were so familiar to him. He just can't remember why.

He shrugs this notion off and gets comfortable in his bed. *Where were we, Yvonne?* Albert thought to himself and fades back in his mind to that pleasure beach in hopes to slide right back in where he left off but there's nothing but random dreams that await him.

For the next two weeks, Albert spends his days at home in his room mostly reading but pining away for Yvonne. He struggles to concentrate upon the novels that he's chosen. Each day would go by and he hoped to go back to that paradise by the beach but each night would come and go and he'd be greeted with nothing but random nonsense. Yvonne wouldn't even be mixed into this.

During his waking hours though he spent nearly every moment contemplating their future together and how he was going to make his dream a reality. In his mind, he still could hear the sounds of the waves crashing against the platinum white sands of the beach.

Finally, the two weeks go by and it's the morning of December 14th. Albert's alarm goes off and his eyes open wide. He throws the covers off of himself and springs forth from his cocoon of blankets a man on a mission. Even if that mission is to go return his library books, his main mission is something far more important. His mission for today is to talk to the lovely Yvonne. Look into those warm light brown eyes of hers and confess his feelings for her.

Albert walks out of his room and across the hall and fixes himself a hot shower. He runs over his game plan in his mind once, twice, twenty times. He reaches out and grabs a dark blue towel off the towel rack and dries off still thinking things over. Once he dries off he wraps the towel around his waist and darts across the hall back into his room. Casting the towel aside, Albert walks towards his closet then throws on a pair of clothes he's had picked out for almost two weeks, a dark red flannel shirt and blue jeans paired with his black and white sneakers.

Albert gets dressed and walks down the hall to the living room. He can hear his mother in the kitchen talking to herself as usual. He creeps closer to the archway leading into the kitchen. He can overhear her lightly praying to herself. He can't make out exactly what she's saying but he hears his name mixed in there followed by her saying "Amen," several times. Albert knocks on the archway. "I'm going out, Ma," he said, walking towards the door.

"Hold on, Albert!" she yells out and comes walking out of the kitchen with her coffee mug in one hand and purse in the other. "Where are you headed off too? Are you going down to the library again?"

"Yes, Ma. I have to return some books and I'm meeting up with Yvonne," Albert said with a grin on his chin.

"Oh, that's great to hear. I was wondering about you two. Have you been calling her?"

Albert rolls his eyes a bit, "Yes, we talk every day."

"OK, Alby. That's good. You really must have her come over for supper some night. I want to meet her!"

"Ma, please don't call me Alby anymore," Albert said.

His mother looks at her watch and frantically replies, "Oh, I'm going to be late! I'm sorry, Alby, we'll talk more tonight when I get home from work," she said, quickly kissing him on the top of his head and bolting out of the house to her car.

Albert lets out a sigh and says to the silence of the house, "You really told her...Alby."

Albert throws his pack full of books on his back, locks the door behind him and brushes off his encounter with his mother. Thoughts of Yvonne quickly cheer him up. He makes his way down the sidewalk and looks up into the clear skies above. *Not a cloud in the sky out today. Wait...spoke too soon.* Albert sees one lone cloud in the sky. "You're not ruining my day ya cloud!" Albert says, shaking his fist at the cloud. Albert looks back down and notices a car passing by him. The driver, an older man, looks at him with a mixture of concern and bemusement. Albert quickly puts his hands in his pockets. His cheeks blush a bright red as he quickly continues along to the LCL.

Albert arrives at the brick pathway leading to the entrance of the Lando Community Library and stops just outside of the doors. He gazes at his reflection in the tinted doors. The light breeze of the day having blown his hair asunder. He quickly straightens it and says to himself, "You got this, man." He takes a deep breath and steps into the warm air of the labyrinth within.

He walks across the shiny linoleum floors reflecting the skylight above. His footsteps echo throughout the open check out area. His eyes scan the area for Yvonne, but all he sees are the usual faces of the library ladies.

"Good morning, Albert!" The familiar voice of Delores travels throughout the area causing the gazes of a few older gentlemen to leave their papers but they quickly look back down to their usual reads of local events.

Albert reaches the counter where Delores stands smiling at him. "Good morning," Albert mumbles to her while sliding his backpack off of his shoulder. He breathes a sigh of relief taking it off. The ten books had weighed him down. He grabs the books and stacks them up on the counter in two piles again.

"So, how did you like them, Albert?" Delores asks while grabbing the books and logging them back into the system.

"Not bad," he said, looking behind Delores into the library office's windows. He sees two of the other library women. The one that stands out is Sheila, a woman in her forties who runs the Teen Advisory Council that Albert used to attend a few years before.

The TAC is a group of high school students who discuss certain group topics and books of the week over light snacks. The main reason Albert attended these meetings was that he was madly in love with a girl who also attended them. A girl named Pat. She had long blonde hair and always wore this checkered cardigan.

He always saw her reading to herself in the back corner of the library. He sat on the other side of the library pretending to read, all the while watching her lightly curl her finger through her hair.

Delores came over to Albert one day when he was in the middle of "reading" and asked him if he was interested in attending a new organization they were creating within the library for teenagers. Albert agreed and then was directed upstairs to a small room where Sheila was setting chairs up. Albert took a seat towards the back, which is where he always sat if given the opportunity.

A few minutes later several other guys came in and sat towards the front and Sheila began chatting them up. Albert crossed his arms and put his head down waiting to see where all of this was leading. The door opened and Albert expected more guys to come walking in towards the front but someone sat down on the opposite end of the back row. Albert's eyes shifted over and Pat was there. Albert quickly looked away and beads of sweat began developing on his brow.

During this meeting, Sheila discussed the creation of the TAC council and how all of them were its first members and the plan for things to come. It all kind of went in one ear and out the other for Albert. He spent the entire meeting much like all the rest he attended stealing glances at Pat and her lavender blonde hair. He imagined he and Pat sitting in the back splitting a plate of cookies and chips and gazing into each other's eyes. Those thoughts always made him smile, then one day Pat disappeared. His heart shattered silently on that seat in the back row. He wondered where Pat ended up, but he never asked anyone if they knew anything.

"Are you looking for something, Albert?" Delores asked looking over her bifocals at him.

Albert quickly looked for an answer. He so desperately wanted to ask her about Yvonne, but couldn't bring himself to ask. "No ma'am. I'm fine," he managed to say and she turned back to her computer screen and finalized her work.

"OK, Mr. Oden, you're all set. Are you going to go get you some more books? We just got some new horror novels this past week from some of your favorite authors."

Albert's curiosity peaked. "Thanks for the information, Delores," he said and walked over to the stacks continuing his search for Yvonne. He stops along the way in the horror section and sees the new selections Delores had mentioned. He comes across one that piques his interest. The title of the novel is *Tigerlily* and the cover depicts a red-haired woman lurking in the shadows watching a man walk alone through a darkened city street. The art is so eye-catching that Albert immediately puts it in his growing stack of books.

Soon Albert finds himself with another ten books. He walks through the stacks and remembers that he wanted to grab one more book to flip through…one he always flipped through when he was there at the library for a while. He turns down the row where the encyclopedias stand, finds the one he's looking for and slides the thick tome in his bag.

A grin spreads across his face but he's upset that he hasn't seen Yvonne yet. *I did get here earlier today than last time. Maybe she'll show up soon*, he thought to himself while gazing at his watch. '1:45' it reads. Albert decided to read while he waited for her. Albert slides his books down into his backpack and walks to the winding staircase leading to the upstairs area where the study rooms and children's library are located. The sun is directly over the skylight now and the warm rays beam down upon him, magnified by the glass above. Albert feels rejuvenated in this light.

He scales the final steps and arrives upon the second floor where a few children can be seen reading brightly colored picture books and one can be seen walking around in the young adult horror section flipping through one of those 'Choose Your Own Ending' books. Albert continues along and reaches his study room and closes the door behind him. He then closes the blinds of the large window. He lays his bulging bag upon the solid wooden desk in the center of the room and decides to flip through his encyclopedia first.

Albert flips through the thick book past topics of no interest to him until he comes upon the pages detailing the anatomy of the human female. Albert's eyes scan over the page taking in every detail. The page has two illustrations of a nude woman from the front and back.

He's looked over this time and time again throughout his teenage years and cannot help but feel the same sense of excitement that he received the very first time he gazed upon it. The same feelings deep inside of him develop and he feels his mouth begin to go dry and his heart race. He imagines Yvonne's face upon the woman's body and he feels these feelings intensify.

As Albert sits there gazing upon the nude illustrations one of the children he saw earlier outside runs past and gazed in at him through the door's small window. Albert quickly closes the encyclopedia and returns it to his backpack. He takes a deep breath, exhales and calms himself. His mouth is dry and sticky like flypaper so he decides to step out for a quick drink downstairs at the water fountain.

He traverses the stairs and makes his way to the water fountain located directly to the left of the main desk. While sucking away at the cool water Albert overhears Yvonne's name in the office behind the main desk. He releases the button stopping the flow of water and steps closer to the side of the main desk trying to listen closer. "Aw, the poor thing caught whatever has been going around here too, eh? I just had it myself earlier last week. I hope I didn't give it to her..."

Delores can be heard saying followed by Sheila's reply of, "I know. Bless her heart. She sounded so sick when she called in earlier. She said she'd try to be in tomorrow but I told her to come back when she felt ready." Albert feels tears well up in his eyes. *My dear sweet Yvonne is sick! How could this have happened?! If only I could nurse her back to health...*

Lost in thought again Albert treks back upstairs along the winding staircase. *He thought about how Yvonne could be lying under piles of sheets in the dark coughing and crying out for help. Crying out for him. He comes bursting into the room throws the drapes open letting in the healing bright light of the sun into the darkened room and throws the sheets off of her. Albert plucks her up from the bed and holds her in his arms tightly. He feeds her spoonfuls of chicken noodle soup with vegetables and slips her some vitamins kissing her on the top of her head.*

When Albert comes out of his thoughts he's standing outside of the library with his pack on his back once again. *Wow, I really lost myself there*, he thought, feeling a little unsettled by this. He looks down at his feet and sees his lime green backpack next to him. He unzips the front flap, reaches in and pulls out one of the books to check the due date. Upon inspection, he sees that it has no fresh due date stamped upon the card wherein. *I walked out here without even checking these books out!*

Albert hastily throws the pack over his shoulder and nearly loses his balance not prepared for the weight. He loses his grip on the pack and it falls onto the bricked path with a loud 'THUD'. He thought to himself, *What the heck is in here?* He gazes inside and sees what's made his pack so heavy. *The encyclopedia! No, I meant to put that back on the shelf!*

Albert picks his pack up by the strap and goes back over to the door and pulls, but it remains firmly shut. Albert cups his hands over the glass and gazes into the library and sees that all of the lights are turned off and everyone has left. He flicks his wrist over and looks at the time. '4:33' his watch reads. *Where did the time go?! How long have I been out here?* Albert thought to himself. *Well, it can't be helped. Looks like I'll just have to come back in two weeks...until then Yvonne.* With that thought, Albert slowly brings his pack over his shoulder and onto his back and makes his way home again. He stares off into the horizon where the sun hangs low, ever slowly slipping further out of sight.

Upon reaching his home Albert unlocks the front door and is greeted with silence and darkness inside. He flips the lamp on directly to the left of the door which casts a warm glow upon the carpeted living room. His gaze fixed upon the family Christmas tree which he had set up the day after Thanksgiving. It was a tradition that he had adopted when he was a young boy. He always set up the tree to look exactly as it had the final Christmas his father had spent with them...before he passed away. He reaches down and grabs the power cord and plugs it into the socket, illuminating the room in a bright spectrum of colors. A smile spreads across his face as he looks upon one of his favorite ornaments. He closes his eyes and thinks back to a precious memory between his father and himself.

*Little Al stood beside the Christmas tree, captivated by an ornament. It was a seashell that contained an adorable smiling alligator that wore a Santa hat. The alligator lay underneath three plastic palm trees. As he stood next to the tree his father noticed and asked him, "What are you staring at, my son?"*

*Little Al, his gaze firmly glued to the ornament, replied, "The alligator needs some sunlight, daddy. It's pretty dark on his little beach."*

*His father chuckled and said, "Well, I'll fix that lickity split!" He reached for one of the Christmas lights encircling the tree, a pink one, and tucked it behind one of the palm trees. Little Al squealed with delight at the newly brightened scene. "It's always sunset for Al the Alligator now," his father said, ruffling Little Al's hair.*

Albert's eyes slowly opened and the smile that had developed on his face slowly faded and was replaced with a look of sadness. A lone tear rolls over the corner of his right eye and down his cheek, falling onto the beige carpet below. He lightly pokes the pink bulb within the shell and another memory comes back to him. This one isn't as clear and precise as the one of him and his father. It's a fragment of something Albert can barely recall.

He recalls a time when he could swear he was going to run away from home and he came back for something important he had forgotten. Certainly, this must have been a dream or something. Why would he try to run away? He dismisses this fragmented memory and turns around and walks towards the kitchen.

He sees a yellow sticky note left by his mother attached to the refrigerator door. He plucks it off and reads, 'Alby, there's some leftover spaghetti from last night in the pot at the bottom of the fridge. I'll be home around 10 tonight. Love you! - Ma'.

Albert's mom worked as a nurse on the outskirts of Lando at this hospital for the mentally unwell called Duke's End. Albert had vague memories of the place although he couldn't quite remember when he'd ever visited there. She began working there when Albert was a kid and, as far as he could remember, had always worked the evening shift.

Leftovers and TV dinners were something Albert had grown quite accustomed to and had even grown fond of…to a certain extent. Whenever his mother would make some of her spaghetti, as she had done the previous night, Albert would always eat as much as he could but there would always be leftovers and Albert had a real distaste for leftover spaghetti. It just wasn't the same warmed up in the microwave.

Albert tossed the note aside onto the counter and opened the door to the fridge. He eyeballed the large container of spaghetti which was about a quarter full of sickly pale noodles mixed with tomato sauce. He grabbed the cold pot out of the fridge and set it upon the faux wooden countertop then grabbed one of the ornate plates from the cupboard and began preparing his supper. The sound of the fork spreading through the cold noodles was almost enough to deter Albert but he pressed on and finished his plate. He placed it in the microwave and gave it a good two minutes to warm up.

He returned the pot to the fridge and walked over to the kitchen window. He stared out at the ghostly moon above which cast a dim light onto the front yard. It was a crescent that hung low in the now dark sky outside.

While looking at the moon Albert wondered to himself if maybe Yvonne was possibly gazing upon it at the same time from somewhere out there in Lando. He then realized she was probably asleep in bed still battling the godforsaken sickness the library ladies had given her no doubt.

The microwave issued a DING! behind him bringing him back to the here and now and he opened its door grabbing the plate and lightly burning his fingertips. He quickly set the plate aside on the counter for a moment and poured himself a glass of soda. Taking a sip of soda he then grabbed the plate of spaghetti and walked out to the dining room table right outside their small kitchen.

It was a circular wooden table with three seats. Albert's seat was on one side of the table, his mother's on the opposite side. One seat for a guest was in the middle, which largely remained empty the majority of the time. Albert set his supper down in his usual place located closest to the kitchen then went over to his backpack he'd left by the door and pulled out *Tigerlily* to do some reading as he forced down his leftovers.

Albert flipped the cover of the book open and turned to the first page. He brought a fork full of noodles up to his mouth and began to eat his supper. He found himself unable to concentrate on the story in front of him though. His attention kept slipping back to what Yvonne might be doing and how he wished he could help her.

He turns towards the window directly next to the table and opens the blinds and stares out onto the back yard. He sees the back deck cloaked in darkness and looks up into the sky at the stars above. He notices his reflection staring back at him sitting there all alone with his supper and an open book going unread. He can't help but feel an overwhelming sense of loneliness at this moment.

Albert quickly finishes his supper and returns his plate and glass to the sink. He washes his dishes and places them in the dish caddy next to the sink and heads off to get ready for bed. Albert picks up his book bag sitting by the door and walks to his room. He gives it a light pitch onto his bed and all of the books come sliding out. One, in particular, catches his eye. It was the encyclopedia again. He walks over and picks it up and slides it under his bed for the time being. He'll have to return it with the rest but for now, it'll have to wait.

Albert continued to go through his days as he had been for the past few weeks. He would awake in the morning to prepare himself for the day and get all dressed up with nowhere to go. He would then spend his time either reading or pining over Yvonne.

He had decided that once these two weeks had passed he was going to bring her a tasty chicken noodle soup made by his mother to the library. He would ask her to make it the night before and he'd take it down to her and confess his feelings for her. This thought kept him going through the holiday season where everyone seemed to be with someone. Albert, on the other hand, felt totally alone.

Christmas morning came and along with it the usual guests. Every year Albert's aunt Lolita, his uncle Harry and his cousin Sydney would come over for Christmas dinner. After dinner they would attend the candlelight Christmas ceremony at church.

Albert found himself woken up to the sound of loud laughter from out in the living room. He recognized it immediately as his aunt's. Albert casually walked over to his door and slipped across the hallway to the bathroom and took care of his usual routine and prepared himself for this burst of social interaction he was glad only occurred a few times a year. He put his social face on and gazed at himself one final time in the mirror. He took a deep breath then flipped the light off and walked towards all the commotion in the living room.

"Hey, boss man. Merry Christmas!" his uncle Harry said to him, sitting down on their couch next to his aunt Lolita.

"Hey, Albert. Good morning!" his aunt Lolita said, cheerily.

"Yeah, good morning. Merry Christmas," Albert said, softly. Albert looked around the living room and wondered where Sydney was and just as this thought was processed Sydney poked Albert's sides waking him up fully.

"MERRY CHRISTMAS, AL!" Sydney yelled, causing Albert to leap at least a foot into the air. "Hahaha! You always do that, Al. I love it!" Sydney laughed, falling into the spare seat next to his parents. His father slapped him on the back of the head and told him to settle down.

Albert's mom peeked her head out from around the corner in the kitchen and said, "Alright, you guys, calm down out there."

Already feeling a bit overwhelmed Albert took a walk to the kitchen and told his mom he was going to go get some light reading in while she finished preparing the honey ham and sides. "Don't be rude to our guests, Albert. Go and spend some time with your family." Albert let out a slight sigh and turned back around knowing her mind wouldn't be changed so he made his way back to the living room and took a seat on the red rocking chair across from the three of them.

"So, what have you been up to lately, Albert? Talking to any good lookin' women?" Sydney asked, grinning. Harry gives him another smack on the back of the head. "What did I do? It's an honest question! I'm just concerned about my cousin here!"

"Now, Syd, I'm sure Albert doesn't wanna talk about his private life with us," Lolita said, rubbing the back of Sydney's head.

Interestingly enough Albert felt this was a conversation he wouldn't mind having. He blushed a bit and spoke up, "Actually I have been." The three of them looked at him wide-eyed and eager to hear more. "I met her down at the library last month. Her name's Yvonne. We've been talking every day for the past few weeks."

Sydney got up and took a walk over to Albert, He slapped him on the back and happily said, "That's my Al. I knew you could do it. I taught him everything he knows."

Harry rolled his eyes at this statement then congratulated Albert and wished the two of them luck and extended his hand. Albert blushed and stood up and took his uncle's hand grasping it firmly. "That's a firm handshake. Her father will appreciate that," Harry said, winking at Albert.

The rest of the morning Albert's anxiety went out the window. Christmas dinner was served shortly later and they all sat down to the round table with their plates. It was a bit cramped, but Albert didn't mind that today. His aunt and uncle, along with Sydney, kept prodding him with questions about Yvonne and how they'd like to meet her. Albert's mother spoke up to this statement and told them to get in line that she was meeting her first. Albert ate his honey ham, mashed potatoes, and dinner roll all the while gleefully answering all of their questions.

After Christmas dinner wrapped up everyone gathered around the brightly lit tree and opened their gifts. Laughter filled the room as Lolita and Albert's mother discussed memories of when they were kids and the mischief they had once gotten into growing up.

They took turns opening one gift each until all the gifts were open. Albert received a new bookshelf to assemble from his uncle Harry and a stack of books from his aunt Lolita and Sydney and among the many clothes and such his mother got for him she also got him a shower radio to use which Albert was quite happy to receive. Albert wasn't hard to buy for in the gift department. Books were always a safe bet as long as they were sci-fi and horror related. Albert thanked his family and headed off to his room to put his things away and to get ready to head out to church.

"So, have you and Yvonne sealed the deal yet?" Albert quickly turned around to find Sydney in his doorway. Sydney slowly came in and closed the door behind him.

"What?" Albert managed to muster.

"Have you sealed the deal?" Albert's eyes went wide and he looked down at his feet, blushing wildly. "I can tell by your reaction that's a no," Sydney said, snickering a bit. "I can tell you anything you wanna know, man. It's been ages since we've hung out. You should give me a call sometime. I know the perfect place we can hit up. It's called The Sexothèque."

Albert looked up at Sydney genuinely perplexed by his offer. "That's the strip club downtown, right? You're still with Victoria, aren't you? Why would you want to go down there?"

Sydney lowered his head, chuckled lightly, and replied, "Oh, Al, I love you, man. Yeah, Vicky and me are still together. Coming up on ten years now. I suppose you could say I've decided to…broaden my horizons."

This statement blew Albert's mind. He'd never desire to be like that. "OK, Syd, I need to get ready…"

Albert tried rushing Sydney out of his room but not without Sydney winking at him and saying, "Give me a call sometime, Al. You won't regret it. We'll catch up and have some fun." Albert shut the door in his face and felt sorry for Sydney's girlfriend Victoria. He then pushed it from his mind and began to think about Yvonne once more while he changed into his Christmas suit.

Later, as Albert attended the candlelight ceremony at their church, he sat on the pew with his family and continued to think of Yvonne and how it'd be sitting here with her and having a family together. This thought made him so very happy. *Just a few more days, my love.*

A smile spread across his face which was illuminated by the candle he was holding onto. The candlelight gave him a bit of a sinister look. His mother glanced over at him and noticed this and gave him a light ribbing, asking if he was OK. He said he was fine, but truthfully he felt a mixture of emotions at this moment. More than anything he was nervous about what lay ahead of him at the library. Come what may though Albert was ready to go and express his love.

So, we find ourselves all caught up with Albert on the bustling uptown streets of Lando. Albert is a man on a mission. He fixes his eyes on the large two-story brown brick building of the "LCL" and waits to cross the road. He stares up into the sky for a moment noticing gathering storm clouds. He looks back across the street to see it safe to cross.

Thoughts of how he's going to approach Yvonne swirl about in his mind as he crosses the road and steps onto the brick pathway leading up to the entrance. He approaches the tinted door and checks out his reflection in the glass. Everything appeared to be in place but he still gave himself a quick once over to be safe. He then snapped his fingers at his reflection and took a deep breath and said to himself, "I'm going in for the kill. Alright, here we go…". Albert opened the door confidently, his head held high, and walked towards the front desk.

He enters the warm air of the library. The scent of the thousands of books comfort Albert and slightly calm his nerves. He begins scanning over the various people scattered about in the main lobby of the library but sees no sign of Yvonne. Thoughts begin creeping into his mind about what happened during his last visit and how he never saw her but Albert quickly hushes these nagging thoughts. He thought to himself, *I'm going in for the kill. I'm doing it. It's gonna happen.*

Albert reaches the front desk and sees Delores in the back office, but she appears to be gossiping again with Sheila. He sees the bell on the top of the counter and under normal circumstances wouldn't dream of bringing his palm down upon it and warrant the gazes from all of the people in the library fixated upon him, but today Albert pays no heed to such anxieties. He brings his palm down upon the bell issuing a rezoning DING! throughout the library's large corridor. Delores turns around with a look of surprise and immediately smiles and waves at Albert. He forces a light smile in return.

"Good afternoon, Albert. You weren't out here long were you? I apologize."

Albert lightly sighed and said, "No ma'am. I just got here. I just had a quick question."

Delores, a bit surprised by Albert's directness, replies, "OK, Albert. What can I help you with?"

Albert's anxiety came rushing back at him at this moment and he very nearly didn't ask what needed to be said, but Yvonne's soft eyes came back to him. He felt a burst of confidence within himself once again and inquired, "I was wondering if Yvonne was working today. I heard she was sick the last time I was here. I just wanted to see if she was feeling better."

Delores smiled and pointed over to the back left corner of the library's first floor. "She's right back there, Albert. That's very sweet of you to be concerned for her." Albert quickly thanked Delores and walked towards the back corner where Delores was pointing.

As he walked along he imagined the scene playing out in his mind just like this...*He turns left at the corner up ahead and there she would be standing sorting out book returns. He approaches her slowly and taps her on the shoulder. Yvonne turns around and is surprised to see him. He smiles at her and presents her with the delicious chicken soup. Yvonne lightly coughs still showing signs of her sickness and tears well up in her eyes. She is overcome with emotion that Albert would perform such a kind gesture. She wraps her arms around him and they embrace one another tightly as the world spins around them fading into darkness until nothing exists but the two of them.*

Albert smiles brightly as this vivid fantasy plays out in his mind. He approaches ever closer and begins to hear the familiar sound of books being returned to their rightful places in the stacks. So far so good. Just as Albert is about to make that fateful left turn to begin his fantasy come to life he hears the sound of Yvonne's soft voice. *Talking to yourself? Another thing we have in common.*

Albert is rooted to the spot a moment later by the voice of another person. He stops at the corner in the middle of this shelf. Yvonne and this other person are located immediately around the corner right within Albert's earshot. He listens more closely and discovers the voice belongs to another guy.

"So, what are you doing tonight? You wanna grab a bite to eat over at Akane Dragon?"

Yvonne giggles lightly. "Sure, Clayton. I get off at five. I could go for some sushi."

"Oh, what am I supposed to do until then, Vonnie? This place is so fuckin' boring."

"Oh, I don't know how about you go read a book and work on your diction."

"I'd like to work my diction on you…" Yvonne giggles at this. Albert can't believe what he's hearing. He can almost feel his heart shattering within himself. That old familiar voice comes back screaming with a vengeance at how all of this was a waste of time just like every other instance in his past.

Albert tries to get a hold of himself, but he becomes lost in his thoughts standing there immediately around the corner from Yvonne and Clayton. What Albert doesn't hear is Yvonne saying that she needs to go to the restroom. Because had he heard her he would have promptly moved in between the stacks and faded into the shadows.

What happened instead was Yvonne walking right into Albert and the two of them falling to the floor. The chicken soup splashed all over the library's brown rug, the side of the shelf, and onto Albert and Yvonne.

"Dude, what the fuck is the matter with you?! What were you doing just standing there like a brick shit house?!" Albert's eyes go wide with horror not realizing exactly what had just occurred. One minute he's vertical the next horizontal with chicken soup drops on the lenses of his glasses. He sits up and to his horror, he sees Yvonne covered in chicken bits and noodles. It would seem that the brunt of the soup had landed upon her.

"It's OK, Clayton. Calm down. It was just an accident." Albert slowly makes his way to his feet bringing the ton of books in his backpack to his side.

"Were you eavesdropping on our conversation, you little shit? Do you get off on listening to couples having private conversations?" Albert's gaze was fixated upon his sneakers now covered in a light yellow film of soup. "Well, say something ya asshole!"

Albert looked up slowly and found Yvonne looking right at him and he just couldn't face any more of what had happened. He promptly took to his heels flinging his pack onto his back once more and made a direct line for the front door. "Albert, wait!" Yvonne calls out from behind him, but he cannot tell if Yvonne truly said it or if it was what he wanted to hear. He hits the door, slamming it open paying no mind to the spectacle he's made of himself.

He enters the cold gray afternoon rushing down the sidewalk wanting to put as much ground between him and this place as he can. A frigid arctic blast of air barrages his face chilling him to the core. The once warm sun shining down before is covered by impending storm clouds. Albert can feel the first drops of water rain down upon him as he crosses the road. He continues at breakneck speed along the sidewalk as the heavens rain down upon him. He finds himself stopping a few blocks from his home when he realizes no one is after him. Soaked to the bone, Albert feels there's no need to run any longer. *What's the rush? What have I got to get back home too?* He continues along the glistening roads walking through freezing ankle-deep water. Albert feels that he just doesn't care anymore.

He reaches his home and opens the door. The house is warm and the lights are all on. Albert slides out of his ruined sneakers tossing them onto the porch along with his socks and closes the door behind him. He throws his backpack down next to the door with a loud THUD.

Albert's mother can be heard lightly singing to herself from the kitchen. "Hi, Alby! I'm making your favorite for supper tonight! I hope you didn't get caught out in this storm! Did you take an umbrella?" Albert certainly has no appetite after the ordeal he just went through. He says nothing and makes his way, still dripping wet, to his bathroom.

He begins slipping out of his clothes when his mother comes rapping on his chamber door. "Are you OK in there?" Albert foolishly ignores her hoping she'd just go away. She instead begins turning the knob and raps harder upon the door. "Albert? Answer me!"

Albert finally out of his dripping wet clothes yells, "I'M FINE!!"

"OK, Albert. You don't need to yell! I was just worried!" He feels a tinge of guilt about yelling at her but doesn't apologize. He says no more to her and he hears the audible sound of her footsteps walking away.

Albert ran a hot shower to warm himself. He stood within the steam and the steady flow of hot water cascading over his body. It failed to revitalize him. He couldn't warm the cold he felt throughout his body. He tries not to think of what happened earlier, but images of Clayton's angry face and Yvonne covered in soup flash in and out of his mind.

He stops the steady flow of hot water upon his battered body and dries himself off then drags himself off to bed. He feels so very cold. He digs out a thick yellow V neck sweater from the bottom of his dresser drawer and his flannel pajama pants to sleep in and crawls under his sheets and passes out in seconds.

Later that night Albert tosses and turns in his bed having vivid fever dreams. One theme kept repeating itself over and over within them. Albert was running down a darkened city street. It wasn't any he was familiar with and every one of the houses he passed had dark windows.

He felt the presence of something after him. It was something hot on his heels but he didn't dare look behind him for he felt if he did he'd surely be caught. He was running as cold sheets of rain fell onto him from the purple alien sky above. The clouds looked as if they had a life of their own and could descend upon him and envelope him in their darkness. Sometimes he would run past the cars scattered about on the street and catch glimpses of a reflection that wasn't his own. This reflection was one he felt a strange familiarity with. It was a woman with bright red hair. As he continued to run he felt each time he saw her reflection that she was trying to say something to him.

He felt the presence of whatever was chasing him growing ever closer behind him. He then began to hear someone yelling, "Wake up!" At first, it was far off in the distance but it grew ever closer, louder as he continued running. "Wake up, Albert!" It became a deafening yell in his ears. He felt his lungs about to burst and he could run no longer. He brought his hands to his ears but the yelling wasn't the only sound he could hear now. The guttural growling of the beast which had been chasing Albert was quickly approaching. He looked over at one of the car windows and could see the reflection of the red-haired one staring back at him. Her eyes were full of concern and Albert felt such warmth emanating from them. She spoke clearly and softly, "Wake up, love."

# Chapter 2
# The Red-Haired One

"Albert?! Wake up, Albert!" His mother was yelling and shaking him. Albert's eyes slowly opened and he could see her standing next to his bed with a frantic look upon her face. "Good lord, Al! I've been here trying to wake you up for the past five minutes! You were tossing around so much and talking nonsense!"

Albert felt like he'd sweated through every stitch of clothing he put on. He threw off his V neck sweater and kicked his sheets off of his legs. "I'm OK, Ma...sorry to worry you. I was just having some...bizarre dreams."

His mother handed him a glass of water that had been on his bedside table. "Here drink this. You need some fluids. I poured it for you right before I came in. I've been watching after you all night. I came in to check on you last night since you didn't come out for supper. You left your door unlocked so I came in and you were sweating bullets. I felt your forehead and you were burning up so I left you to sweat out the fever...which..." she took her right hand and put it onto Albert's forehead, "your fever seems to have finally broken."

Albert sat up in his bed and looked at his watch. '8:08' the digital watch read. "Man, I've been out for a long time."

His mother shook her head at him. "Yes, and you still need to be. You're still unwell. I found the clothes you wore yesterday. I had no idea you walked home in the freezing rain! You should have called me to come and pick you up or asked Yvonne for a ride!"

Albert winced at the mention of Yvonne and lied back down turning over facing towards the wall. "Look, Ma. I'm sorry to worry you like this. Just let me rest."

"OK, Alby…you drink your water. I'll bring you some juice and chicken soup later."

Albert winced even more at this. "No, Ma. How about some vegetable soup or something. Anything but chicken soup…"

"OK. Whatever you want. You just rest yourself and focus on getting better," she said, leaving him alone once more.

Albert lies in his bed thinking about the dream that he'd had. It had already begun to fade from his mind. He couldn't shake the feeling of fear he had felt but also the immeasurable feeling of love he had felt from that red-haired woman. "Good God what a dream," Albert mumbled to himself as he turned over grasping for the glass of cold water. He sipped slowly on it. The cool liquid coursed down his throat and felt pleasant in his warm stomach. The glass was already as sweaty as he was. He turned back over and shut his eyes and began drifting back to sleep.

He didn't have much else to do except lie there in his darkened room. In the brief moments after he awoke, when he didn't remember what had transpired a few days before, he felt fine. It wasn't long before he felt the same hopelessness creeping back into his mind though. He wanted to get better, but he also questioned the point of it. Who cared if he did, excluding his mother of course. That thought wasn't very comforting to him though.

Albert spent the better part of the next two days in and out of darkness and sleep. He would wake up for a while and be alone with his thoughts. He stared up at the walls for hours and lost all track of time until he found himself drifting off to sleep once more.

It went on like this until Albert found himself awoken to the sound of a familiar voice. "Yo, Al, you alive in here?" Sydney said. Albert turned his bedside lamp on and sat up in his bed. His hair a matted mess of tangles falling slightly into his eyes. He felt caked in sweat and dirt. "You look like shit, bro," Sydney said, stifling a laugh.

Albert rolled his eyes at him. "Thanks...What do you want, Syd? Can't you see I'm trying to sleep? It's..." Albert looked at his watch. "Oh, lord. Is it six o'clock?"

"In the PM. You know it, Al," Sydney said, smiling.

Albert smiled lightly. Something he hadn't done in what felt like a very long time. "What brings you over, Syd?"

Sydney took a seat at Albert's reading desk in the corner of his room. "Well, I heard you haven't been feeling well, Al. I just wanted to come over and see how you've been doing…I was thinking of inviting you out with me to The Sexothèque tonight."

"What about Victoria? I thought you'd be ringing in the new year later with her," Albert said, his eyes wider and more awake now.

"There's nowhere saying I can't do both. I'm going out for a few hours then going back to our place. It'll be fine."

Albert kind of made a face at this statement but said nothing further on the subject of Victoria. "I appreciate the thought but I'm not interested."

Sydney shuffled his feet a bit then sighed. "Is it Yvonne? Look she doesn't have to know about it. It'll be our little secret, my main man."

Albert averted his gaze from Sydney. "No, it has nothing to do with…her. I just want to stay here. I'm still not well. I can't go out gallivanting at The Sexothèque. I'm liable to relapse."

Sydney stood up and walked over to the door. "I understand, bro. I kinda figured you wouldn't but I had to ask. Hey, I have a better reason for coming over here. I've got a surprise for you. Call it a late Christmas present." Before Albert could inquire what this surprise was, Sydney was already out the door, running down the hallway.

He could hear Sydney talking to his mother out in the living room. He overhears Sydney say something about, "I hope Al enjoys this." and his mother saying, "Oh, it's very sweet of you to think of Al. I know he will." Albert throws his legs over the side of his bed and into his house shoes and begins to walk towards his half-open door when he hears heavy footsteps walking down the hallway towards his room. He sits back down on the side of his bed and awaits whatever this surprise may be.

Albert's door opens slowly and he sees his mom's bright cheery face smiling at him. "Well, good evening, sleepyhead. You slept the day away." Albert's mother slowly comes into his room. Behind her, he can see Sydney holding onto something he can't quite make out in the darkened hallway. It looks like a box. Whatever it was it was a bit heavy causing Sydney to make those heavy footsteps that Albert had heard. Sydney came into Albert's room and set his surprise down upon Albert's reading desk. In the light of his bedside lamp, Albert could finally see just what it was that Sydney had brought to him.

"A television set?" Albert said, looking at Sydney and his mother who both had grins on their faces. Albert's face didn't match theirs, however.

"Well, Al, what do ya think?" Sydney asked, grinning.

Albert crossed his arms and glared at the clunky box of a television set sat upon his reading desk, "I don't care much for television. I prefer books." Sydney's grin quickly faded.

Albert's mom spoke up, "Oh, Albert, Sydney brought this over here just for you. Don't be grouchy."

Albert sighed at this remark, "I'm not being grouchy. You know I have a whole stack of books to read as it is. I don't have time to rot my brain with mindless television."

"Pile of books?" Albert's mother quickly walked out of his room down the hallway and grabbed Albert's backpack he had left sitting by the front door. She quickly walked back up the hallway and returned to Albert's room. "You mean this pile?" She lay the backpack on the floor in the middle of the room and unzipped it. She pulled out the remains of several of the books within the pack including the warped remains of *Tigerlily*. All Al could make out on the cover was the brilliant red hair of the woman in the shadows. It hurt Al to see the books in such a state and he motioned for her to put them away.

"OK. I guess I don't have a pile of books to read...you got me there. I'm still not fussy on the TV though."

Sydney laid his hand on the television set. Rubbing the side of its faux wood paneling he said, "This baby here was my very first TV set. I've had it for ten years and it's seen me through quite a boring night, Al. Mom and dad ended up getting me another one for Christmas as a kind of housewarming gift for me and Vicky for our new apartment. I didn't know what to do with this one then I thought of you being over here all by your lonesome. Please, Al. Can you give her a good home?"

Albert looked into Sydney's eyes and swore he could see tears forming in the corners of them. He could refuse no longer. "OK, Syd. You win. I'll give 'her' a good home."

Sydney looked over to Albert and the grin came back once more. "Really? Thanks, Al. I know you'll enjoy her as much as I did." He walked over, slapped Albert on the back and hugged Albert's mother tightly. Sydney looked at his silver wristwatch, "I'll leave you to it then, Al. I know I just got here, but hello, I must be going!" Sydney waved goodbye to them and quickly ran down the hallway and out the door. They could hear his car start and seconds later he was gone. Albert's gaze went back to the television set. His reflection looked back at him from the glass of the picture.

"Do you want me to help you set up your new TV, Alby?" his mother said, grabbing the power cord and going to plug it in.

"Do I have a choice?" Albert said under his breath.
"What did you say?" his mother said, half paying attention to him.

"Nothing, Ma." She continued to fumble around underneath Albert's reading desk until she finally located the outlet. Albert stood behind her watching as she plugged it in and came out from under his desk.

"Would you like to do the honors?" she asked, smiling that bright smile again.

"Sure. Why not." Albert said, pulling the power/volume knob out. They both stood there waiting for the darkened picture to light up with the expected white snow but as they continued to stand there the picture continued to remain black.

"Hmm, that's odd." Albert's mother muttered. "Let me see if I got it in there all the way." She crouched down and pressed the power cord further into the outlet even though it was clear to Albert it was securely plugged in. Albert pushed the power knob back in and pulled it out once more and they continued to wait, but it continued to sit, lifeless.

"Oh, no wonder Syd wanted to give it away. The bloody thing doesn't even work!" Albert said, highly displeased that he now was stuck with this thing in his room. "No wonder he took off so fast. Give 'her' a good home indeed!" Albert continued to vent.

"Well, it is the thought that counts I suppose…maybe he didn't know? Maybe it just needs a while to warm up? Leave it on, Alby, and maybe it'll come on."

Albert rolled his eyes at this suggestion but shrugged his shoulders. "OK, Ma. Thanks for the help." He looked down at his backpack, the books still partly visible. "Could you throw out these books? I'll never be able to decipher them. It hurts to say that. I was so looking forward to reading them."

"Sure thing. You get some more rest if you need it. Later on tonight we can watch the ball drop in Times Square."

"Alright, Ma. I'm going to lie back down…"

"OK, Alby." Albert's mother went in to kiss the top of his head then stopped and said, "Pew, you need to take a shower later. You're a little ripe."

"Gee, thanks, Ma." Albert's mother left him, closing the door behind her.

Albert sat upon his bed and glanced over at the television set. It sat there almost mocking him. *Nothing ever works out for me it seems*, Albert thought as he went over to inspect the set further. He turned it around and read the manufacturer sticker on the back. 'Manufactured March 1988' it read. "Almost 10 years old, huh? Still hope for it I suppose," Albert said to himself. He walked back over to his bed and turned his bedside light off and dove back into bed.

He lied on his back, alone with his thoughts again. Thoughts of everything he didn't want to think of came back to haunt him as they had been for days now. He reflected upon his feelings towards Yvonne and his ever-present search for *the one*. The one to take him away from all of this. The one to fill his life with never-ending happiness and purpose.

He began to think to himself that maybe such a thing didn't exist within this world. That possibility was the one that not only brought him to tears but made him weep. He wept loudly into his pillow so his mother wouldn't hear. He wept harder than he had in a very long time. Tears flowed freely from him until he cried himself to sleep.

Hours passed and Albert slept through his mother's knocking to wake him up to watch the New Year's festivities. He slept through the constant booms of fireworks from the yearly New Years Eve fireworks show over Lake Lethe. He slept through everything until a certain television decided to finally illuminate his darkened room with snowy light.

Albert's eyes slowly opened. The flood of tears dry on his cheeks was cold beneath the underside of his face pressed onto his pillow. He flipped his pillow over onto the dry cool opposite side and then realized his room was illuminated in a ghostly white glow.

He sat up in his bed looking at the television. *Well, looks like Ma was right. I guess it just needed some time to warm up*, Albert thought, continuing to gaze upon the picture transfixed by the dancing snow when he began to notice the sound of what he thought at first must be the static hiss from the television. What was strange was that it wasn't constant. It rose and fell. Listening closer to it he could swear it sounded like waves crashing against a beach then receding then crashing back upon the shoreline once again.

Albert thought this sound was quite soothing and lay back down listening to the crash of these "waves". He had no idea how the TV was producing such a sound but he just lay there listening. He shut his eyes and imagined a beach he had dreamed of not long ago. A beach with platinum white sand and palm trees next to a bay of bright crystal clear water. Albert could swear the sound was becoming more and more ocean-like.

He felt his imagination must be running away with him again because he swore he heard the sound of a seagull squawking along with the waves. He opened his eyes to see his room bathed in not the ghostly white glow from before but a beautiful warm pink glow. He sat up in his bed and was astonished to see the picture wasn't snow anymore, but of the beach he had just imagined in his mind's eye. He sat there dumbfounded watching the crystal clear water crash against the platinum sand.

One thing he hadn't pictured though was the wooden backed beach chair sat upon the sand beneath a large black and white striped umbrella. Sat upon this chair was a person faced towards the bay. Her head was obscured by a large straw sun hat. Albert couldn't explain it but he knew it was a woman. He continued watching her amazed at the sharpness of the picture. She moved her hands to the oversized sun hat and removed it slowly. The back of her short red hair immediately caught Albert's eye. The curvature of her neck glistened in the pink light of the setting sun on the horizon.

She turned slowly, the breeze off of the bay lightly blowing her long brilliant bangs over her left eye. A sly smile formed upon her face. Albert felt almost voyeuristic. She turned her face more and Albert could finally see her right eye, dark brown much like his own and he almost felt like she was…looking at him.

"You like what you see, Albert?" Albert's eyes grew wide. *No, I couldn't have heard that. This is quite the show. Maybe Ma came in and hooked up the cable or something while I was asleep,* Albert told himself. "This isn't a show, Albert," the woman said, speaking clearly. The waves didn't drown her out at all.

She moved her long legs over to the side of the chair and Albert could see she was wearing a navy blue blazer with what looked like a black tank top underneath, bright yellow pants, and black loafers with bright red socks. "This is your world. As far as your eyes can see. You created all of this." *How can I hear her so clearly? It's as if she's speaking to me in my mind.* She began to giggle to herself lightly. "Love, I am in your mind. I suppose I don't need to move my lips here, but speaking to you normally is what I felt would be the wiser choice at this time."

*I must be dreaming. Yeah, that's it. I must have passed out again listening to that static from the television*, Albert assured himself. "I can assure you, love, that this isn't a dream. Not this time." Albert, still unbelieving, brushed off this statement and moved further down his bed closer to the TV. The two remained still, watching each other. He watched as the breeze continued to lightly tousle her hair. She lifted her right hand and ran her hand through it moving it out of her face smiling at him. Albert smiled back at her and finally spoke. "Who are you?"

She looked him right in the eye and said, "I'm your dream girl, Albert. I'm, how did you put it? *'the one'*." Albert recalled his profound sadness from before. *How...how did she know about that? This dream is so vivid. I could swear it's not a dream, but what other explanation is there?* Albert tried to rationalize what was happening to him. "I told you this isn't a dream, love. I know! I'll prove it to you. I'll be here tomorrow at this exact time." Albert looked down at his watch. It read '2:46'. "I'll be here at 2:46, love. I'll be counting down the hours..." As she finished speaking the picture began to fade to snow.

"Wait, what's your name?!" Albert yelled out.

"She stood up and with a grin said, "My name is Elly."

Just like that, she was gone. The television screen was nothing but a blizzard of static snow. Albert sat there staring into the screen for a few minutes thinking about Elly and how crazy everything that had just happened was. He was unsure of whether it all happened but couldn't shake what Elly had told him. 'I'll be here at 2:46, love.' Love…my how that made him feel happy. No one had ever called him that before. *My dream girl, eh?* He lay there in the ghostly lit room with a grin on his face then everything faded to black as Albert fell into a deep sleep.

Albert awoke the next morning to the sound of knocking on his door. His eyes slowly opened and he could see his mother across the room turning the knobs upon his television set. "What are you doing, Ma?"

"Happy New Year, sleepyhead. I was just trying to get this thing to work. It's still not coming on," she said, continuing to turn each knob.

Albert sat up slowly, the events of the previous night coming back to him in fragments. "Wait, it's not working again?"

"Was it working last night?" his mother said, turning towards him, giving up on her fruitless effort to bring life to the set.

"Yes...at least I think so," Albert said, genuinely unsure if the events he recalled had occurred or he was recalling an extremely vivid dream.

"Well, Alby, it's not working now and the knobs were exactly where I left them yesterday evening." Albert looked down at his bed and thought to himself that everything WAS just a dream. Of course, it was. Sydney had given him a bum television set and he had had quite the vivid dream.

Albert's mother was still messing with the dials and checking the power cord when he hopped out of bed. He slid his feet into his soft navy blue house shoes and walked over to her. He lay a hand upon her shoulder and said, "It's time to call it, Ma. Sydney offloaded a bum T.V. onto me. You can stop fooling around with it."

Albert's mother frowned and looked at the T.V. defeated. "I guess so...maybe you can figure out the problem, Alby." He walked her over to his door when she said to him, "Hey, would you like to go out for lunch today? It's New Year's Day and I'd like to go out and ring in the new year before my shift tonight since you were passed out last night. I tried waking you but you were so snug I didn't wanna disturb you."

"I...suppose we can. I mean I've been cooped up in here for about a week. I do need some fresh air."

His mother lit up at this. "Oh, that's great. It's been a while since we've been out on the town. How about some Chinese today? We can go down to Akane Dragon?"

Thoughts of Yvonne came creeping back into his mind when she mentioned that. What if he should run into her or even worse Clayton? He looked at his mom and her face was full of happiness. Albert begrudgingly agreed to go out. "One thing, Alby, can you hop in the shower? You're kinda ripe." On that note, his mother left out to get ready. *I guess I do need a shower...* he thought to himself. He scratched his cheek a bit and could feel the stubble upon his face. *...and a close shave.* He walked across the hallway to the bathroom.

Once in the bathroom, he looked at himself in the mirror. What he saw was quite the sight. His hair was an oily mess. His face was covered in a week's worth of beard stubble. It drove him crazy to see himself in this way.

He slipped out of his sleep clothes and took a much-needed shower. He lathered and scrubbed days upon days of built-up sweat and tears he'd amassed during this hellish week. He stepped out of the bathtub and shaved off the five o'clock shadow from his face. He always preferred keeping his face smooth and neat much like the rest of his appearance. He finished up in the bathroom then went back to his room and began to get dressed.

He threw on a green-colored t-shirt with a black cardigan and some blue jeans. It wasn't extravagant. All Albert wanted was to get a bite to eat and enjoy the day with his mother. A knock came upon the door followed by his mother's voice, "You ready, Alby? I'm hungry."

"Yeah, Ma. Just let me get my shoes on." He slipped his feet into his favorite pair of loafers and opened the door.

His mother was waiting in the hallway standing against the wall wearing a floral-patterned dress with knee-high black boots. "Oh, you look nice, Alby."

"Thanks, Ma. Let's go."

"Oh, brush your hair, Alby. It's all over the place and take your vitamin, sweetie." Albert sighed and stepped into his bathroom closing the door behind him. He quickly opened the cabinet and combed through his hair. He looked at himself in the mirror and was satisfied. He went for his vitamins next, but as he was about to open the container he decided he'd take one later. He didn't want them to give him a bad stomach or anything since he'd not eaten anything in days. After returning everything to the cabinet Albert came out and they walked down the hallway towards the front door.

Albert opened the door and stepped out onto the front porch followed by his mother. He looked up into the bright blue cloudless sky. It was the polar opposite of how it looked the last time he was outside. He stood there breathing deep of the crisp fresh air while his mother locked the door. "Ready?" she said to him, smiling. He nodded his head and they both walked over to the car.

Albert's mother drove a Buick Skylark from the mid-80s. It had been their family car for a long time now. Albert had many memories of playing in the back seat with his toys and sticking random stickers onto the back window, some of which were still present. Albert may have grown up but he still enjoyed sitting back there.

His mother opened the driver's side door and reached in and opened the back seat for Albert. They both slid onto the soft seats, shut the doors, and took off for Akane Dragon. Albert looked out the window, gazing at the scenery pass by.

As they drove along he thought back to the television set. He had a nagging feeling he couldn't dismiss that what happened last night couldn't all have been a dream. *Certainly, the television was on. Was it not? It felt SO real. I'll take a look at the thing when I get back home. Maybe Ma didn't have the knob turned far enough to turn it on? She and technology never have mixed well.*

Akane Dragon wasn't too far from their home and they arrived before he knew it. He decided to put a pin in that thought and would come back to it after he'd had a nice meal. He exited the car, the soft seats squishing beneath him, and the two walked to the entrance. Albert could smell the food from the parking lot and was already fully famished when they arrived inside to the counter waiting to be seated. One of the workers, an Asian man with glasses, came over and asked, "Just two?"

His mother answered, "Yes, just two."

"OK, right this way," he answered and led them to a booth by one of the restaurant's large ornate circular windows looking out upon the walkway to the front entrance and the road they'd driven on to get there. On the other side of the road were a string of other businesses: a pawn shop, a bakery, a video store among others stretching further down the street and out of sight.

Albert slid into the booth sitting across from his mother and the man asked what they would like to drink. Albert's mother ordered a Pepsi and Albert ordered a 7 Up. They then walked over to the buffet and began to load up their plates with various foods. Albert got his usual; chicken fried rice, lo mein noodles, fried shrimp, honey chicken, stuffed crab, lemon pepper chicken wings, and some sushi. He sat down first and began eating.

His mother sat down and looked over at another woman sitting at a table across from them. "Trini? Hey, girl! How's it going?" his mother said, waving to the woman at the other table. Albert looked over and saw a young woman sitting at the booth with her two kids and husband. The woman waved back and her two kids looked over at Albert and his mother. His mother continued to carry on a brief conversation as Albert kept his head down and ate trying to ignore her until she went on to say, "This is my son Albert.". Albert looked up, noodles hanging out of his mouth, He sucked them in and nodded at all four of them looking at him now.

"These are my two. Danny and Corey. Danny's the oldest. You haven't met my husband either. This is Tommy," the woman went on as her husband sat there eating much like Albert trying to ignore this back and forth. She lightly nudged him and he looked up and waved. They chatted for another few minutes when the woman and her family got up and got ready to go.

"It was good seeing you, Trini."

"You too, Milly." They waved bye to each other and finally, Albert's mother began to eat her food.

"Milly?" Albert said, stifling a laugh.

"Yes, that's what my friends call me, Alby. I know her from the bank. She works there as a teller."

"Ah, I see. OK, then. You better get to eating, Ma. Your food must have gotten a bit cold by now."

"It'll be fine," she said, digging into her plate.

Albert went back up to the buffet, made another plate, and returned to the booth. "So, how's work been, Ma?" he said to her. He hadn't been able to talk much with her this past week and wanted to catch up a bit.

"Things have been going well. The usual. I enjoy my job, but some of the people I take care of are pretty pitiful. Makes me sad sometimes."

Albert shook his head and looked out the window at the passing traffic. She went onto explain some of the newer people she'd been caring for and how some were separated from reality. Albert nodded again but began to tune her out.

He wanted to listen but his thoughts were on something else. A red-haired woman named Elly to be precise. He looked down at his watch '2:15' it read. *Hmm, twelve hours to wait. I highly doubt that. Dream girls are nothing but that...Dreams.* Albert's mother continued to talk about her job completely oblivious that Albert was miles away.

Having filled their stomachs, both Albert and his mother finished up at Akane Dragon and made their way back home. Albert was relieved he didn't see any familiar faces of his own during his time out with his mother. He could go the rest of his life and be happy not running into anyone from that day at the library again.

Once they arrived back home Albert slipped out of his clothes hanging everything back up within his closet right where he got them from. Tidiness and order was the law of the land for Albert. Once everything was put away and he had slipped into his lounging clothes again, he set his eyes upon the television.

He looked under his desk and checked to see if the power cord was indeed plugged in properly. Yes, it was. He noticed the power knob was already out. *So, this thing was on the entire time we were out.* He pushed the knob back in and waited a minute then pulled it back out. He waited for the screen to light up but again it remained black as it had the previous evening. He turned the volume up and placed his ear by the speaker listening for anything that might be coming out. All he heard was silence.

There was nothing more Albert could do here. He left the TV on in the off chance it might come on and lied down upon his bed and began to think about Elly again. He had a feeling that he had seen her somewhere before. It was a feeling he couldn't shake. He wished he could remember but all he could recall was the previous night and how he'd seen her crystal clear upon the television screen. It didn't even look like a screen but more of a…portal. A portal to another realm.

Albert's evening was spent much the same as they usually were. His mom headed off to work a twelve-hour shift at Duke's End around six that evening. She kissed his head goodbye much to Albert's dismay and left Albert all alone in the house. Usually, Albert would enjoy these quiet hours alone, joyfully soaking up a novel he'd checked out from the library, but his usual plans were thwarted. All of his new books were ruined. The only silver lining to the whole bloody affair was that Albert wouldn't be charged for them. They had no idea he had taken them and he certainly wasn't going to be telling them either. He felt like he'd never return to the library. After that debacle how could he ever show his face down there again?

Albert found himself having to choose one of his old books again from his bookshelf. He chose one he'd read hundreds of times at least and began to read it on the couch. He got as far as a hundred pages in when his eyes began to grow heavy. He had slept so much the night before, yet he found himself so bored he was falling asleep. He decided to call it a night around nine o'clock and returned the book to his shelf, brushed his teeth, and slipped into bed. Once his head hit the pillow he immediately fell asleep.

From the depths of Albert's sleep, a voice began to speak to him, "Love? Looove? It's time to wake up, Albert." Albert's eyes slowly opened and his eyes began to adjust to the golden light that filled his room. It was as if the sunlight he basked in earlier that afternoon was shining into his room, but it wasn't coming from his window. No, his window was dark. He looked down upon his watch, '2:46' the cold digital numbers read, illuminated in the glowing teal-colored backlight. *Wait…2:46? Elly said she'd be back here then!*

And just as that thought left his mind a voice spoke to him, "Yes, love, and here I am." In his sleepy state Albert hadn't realized that the light filling his room was coming from the television set. On the television, Elly sat on a wooden lounge chair on a balcony overlooking the bay he'd seen before. The sun hung high in the sky, a golden orb basking everything in a brilliant light.

"I promised you I would be back, Albert. I hated to wake you, but I wanted to show you that you weren't dreaming. THIS is real, Albert," she said, pointing out to the bay and the platinum beach that stretched as far as the eye could see. The palm trees were lightly swaying in the breeze coming off of the crystal clear water and Albert could swear he smelled the salty fragrance of the sea. He could lightly hear the sound of the waves down upon the beach as well. Albert sat there for what felt like forever unable to take his eyes off of the beautiful scenery.

"Albert? Are you OK? Do you understand, love?" Albert's eyes shifted from the beautiful scenery to the even more breathtaking beauty of Elly. He quickly averted his eyes looking down at his bedsheets. "Oh, Albert. You don't need to be shy around me. There's no need for that. Look at me, love." Albert's eyes slowly glanced up and the two of them locked eyes together. He continued to look into Elly's dark brown eyes as she looked into his. He felt like averting his gaze again, but he didn't.

Instead, Albert noticed that she had changed her outfit from the night before. Tonight she was wearing a black and white striped double-breasted blazer with an orange button-up shirt underneath that matched her vibrant red hair which was slicked back. To the left of her mouth was a light brown mole previously hidden by her hair. One thought came to his mind, *Cute mole.* "Thanks, love," Elly said, a large smile forming on her face. This time Albert *did* avert his gaze, but only for a moment.

"How did you wake me?" he said, looking back up.

Elly smiled, "You and I are connected, love. When you're sleeping the connection is stronger. I just concentrated and thought of your face and focused my thoughts on reaching you. I'd never quite reached you that way before, but it just felt like something I could do. I can't explain it. It's just something I've always been able to do."

Albert's brow furrowed at this. "What do you mean exactly? How are we connected?"

Elly stood up then walked to the edge of the balcony. She looked out upon the bay. The sun hung further down in the sky now casting a slightly pinker glow. She had a deep look of contemplation upon her face. "This is a lot to take in. I don't want to throw all of this upon you at once, love. I promise you we'll discuss all of this in time." Albert understood from the look upon her face that this wasn't an easy question to discuss and he couldn't argue that all of this *WAS* a lot to process. He believed her when she said that this wasn't a dream. Albert had quite the imagination but nothing quite like this.

"Love, we should call it a night here. I want you to rest and think about all of this. Now that you understand this is real I feel you need some time to process it."

Albert sat there a second and spoke up. "I suppose I do need to think about all of this…but when can I see you again?"

Elly smiled and replied, "How about tomorrow night at one? We'll make it a bit earlier this time."

Albert smiled back at her and replied, "That works for me."

Elly turned and began to walk inside of the large mansion the balcony was attached to. Before she walked inside she turned around and winked and said, "I'll be thinking of you, Albert." She then slowly walked inside closing the double glass doors behind her as the picture became more and more filled with snow.

Albert found himself staring at that old familiar blizzard again and flew back onto his pillow thinking to himself, *I'll be thinking of you too, My Elly.* He felt something stir deep inside of him then. It was something he hadn't felt in a very long time. When he had called her, 'My Elly', an old familiar feeling of nostalgia came over him. *Something's going on. Oh, Elly. I can't wait to see you again*, he thought as his eyes grew heavy and sleep came to take him away.

He awoke the next morning to the sound of clanging coming from the kitchen. He stretched and hopped out of bed slipping his feet into his slippers. He opened his door and walked down the darkened hallway towards the living room.

He could hear his mother moving about in the kitchen and softly talking to herself. He peeped around the corner at her and could see she was beginning to make herself some breakfast. "Good morning, Alby! Did I wake you? I was trying to be quiet in here. One of the pans fell out of the cupboard."

Albert shook his head, "No, you didn't wake me. I was going to get up anyway. You must have just gotten home." He looked at the clock on the stove. It's green letters read '7:30'.

"Yes, I was hungry. I was gonna make some bacon and eggs, dear. Would you care for some?"

"I'd love some, Ma. I'm famished. I haven't eaten since yesterday!"

Her eyes went big, "Really? What were you up too last night? You go to bed early? Did you get your television working after?"

Albert sat down to the dining room table in his usual spot. "…Yeah, I did."

"Oh, yeah? That's wonderful. You see? Syd didn't give you a bum T.V. after all." Albert thought about Sydney's charitable donation. "You'll have to thank him when you see him again," his mother said, peeking around the corner at him.

"Oh, yeah. Syd did something great for me." *REALLY GREAT*, he thought to himself, a large smile forming on his face.

He opened the blinds letting the soft morning light cascade over the round dining table. He sat there looking out at some blackbirds sitting in the bare tree in the backyard. They flew away a few moments later, squawking loudly. He felt he could just about fly away into that light blue sky outside. As he sat there thinking about Elly his mother sat a plate of bacon and eggs in front of him and a glass of orange juice. Albert continued to sit, staring out the window. When his mother returned with her plate Albert was still sitting there with the same grin on his face. "Albert? What are you thinking about? Your food's gonna get cold."

Albert was brought back from his thoughts. He looked down at his plate. "Thanks, Ma." He began to eat, looking out the window once again.

"Alby, what are you thinking about?"

Albert shifted his gaze to his mother sitting across from him at the table. "Huh?" he muttered.

"You just look like you've got something happy on your mind."

"Oh, you know…Just stuff. Thinking about something I saw last night."

"You watch something on T.V., Alby?"

He grinned, "Yeah, I did."

"What did you look at?" his mother asked, dipping her bacon into the yolk of her eggs.

"It was…a show about a beautiful beach."

His mother dropped her fork onto her plate. He turned to look at her. "Oh, I'm sorry, Albert. It slipped out of my hand." She picked up her fork wiping off the runny yolk that had covered it. "Um, have you taken your vitamin today?" she asked with a look of concern on her face.

"I will after I eat, Ma."

"Good. I don't want you to get sick again." Albert thought it was odd of her to ask him about that as he was trying to tell her about what he had seen during the night. He wanted to tell her more, but he thought he'd wait for now.

Albert finished up his food then put his dishes in the sink. "Thanks for the food, Ma," Albert said, hugging her tight as she sat there with that concerned look still on her face.

"You're welcome, Albert. I'm going to go get some sleep soon. I had a long night. If you watch your T.V. just keep the volume down, dear."

"OK, Ma. I won't make any noise out here either," he said, smiling.

"Have a good day, Albert."

"I will, Ma."

He entered his bathroom and decided to have a shower and a shave. As he showered he lightly sung to himself, thinking about Elly as he scrubbed his body. He wondered how it would be to have her scrub his back. That thought made him blush and smile brightly. He tried not to laugh but a few chuckles came out. He didn't want his mother to overhear him. He finished up his shower and dried off.

He stepped out onto the blue fuzzy shower rug leaving footprints within it as he moved towards the mirror. He ran the razor over his cheeks shaving off the stubble bit by bit until his face was smooth again.

He looked at the bottle containing his vitamins. He felt strange looking at it. Usually, he just grabbed the bottle and popped a pill and was done with it. He never really looked at the bottle. Albert felt amazing. He decided he didn't need any assistance from some vitamin to keep him healthy. *Vitamin E* was the only vitamin Albert knew he needed. With that thought, he closed the cabinet and went to get dressed.

He entered his room and closed the door behind him, tossing his towel onto his bed. He walked over to his drawers and pulled out some blue plaid boxers and white socks. He slid the socks onto his feet and slid into the boxers then he fell onto his bed. He stretched out and put his hands behind his head.

He began to think about Elly once more and found himself lost in his daydream. He imagined every detail of her face and what it would be like to kiss that adorable mole. Albert spent the rest of the day spread out upon his bed daydreaming about Elly and every little detail he could remember.

Soon the sun began to set outside of Albert's window, but he was still lost in his thoughts. He didn't notice his mother leaving for work later that evening either. She tried to come into his room to kiss his head goodbye but he had firmly locked it and was deeply lost in his thoughts still when she came to say goodbye.

It was around midnight that Albert finally came out of his daydream mainly due to the fact he hadn't eaten in over twelve hours. His stomach started growling and he was jarred from his thoughts. He was imagining walking hand in hand down the platinum white sands of that beach with Elly. Her hand, so soft and warm, within his.

He shook his head amazed at how much time had passed. *Wow, have I been lying here THIS long?* He shrugged. *Time well spent if you ask me*, he thought to himself as he stretched his limbs, hearing a few cracks come from some of his bones and then hopped out of bed.

He walked out of his room into the darkened hallway and could immediately feel a bit of a cold draft from the front door. *Must be pretty cold out there tonight.* He was thankful he didn't have to go out there. He was warm and comfy in his house.

He went to the kitchen and made himself a ham sandwich. He grabbed a bag of potato chips and a can of soda to complete the meal. He sat down to the table and ate his meal in silence periodically checking his watch. He was waiting for 1:00 to roll around. It was almost time. *Another half-hour*, he thought. He quickly finished his meal and washed the plate he had used. The cold tan tile beneath his feet could be felt through his socks and it was chilling him. He ran back into his room and closed the door, firmly locking it behind him. He decided to pull his chair out from his desk and sat right in front of the television set.

He waited as patiently as he could. He shifted back and forth in his seat. He found it hard to sit still so he stood up and paced around the room a bit. During this time he kept a close eye upon his watch. The seconds ticked by agonizingly slow. As excruciating as the wait was, 1:00 finally came. Albert quickly took his seat again, and right at the stroke of 1:00, the television came on by itself. The familiar blizzard is what Albert first saw but it gradually began to clear up and he could see a metal table within the middle of a beautiful garden. Sat down at this table, a clear bubbly drink with a lime hanging on the rim of the glass in front of her, was Elly. She took a sip of the drink then turned slowly facing Albert. A smile formed in the corner of her mouth. "I see you've been waiting for me, love…Nice boxers." Albert quickly looked down and realized he hadn't put any clothes on. He quickly grabbed his towel off of his bed, still damp from his shower. Elly began to laugh. "Love, you don't need to cover up. My, my, how cute you are." He immediately began to blush and averted his eyes for a moment. He threw the towel back onto his bed and sat up straight.

"Hello, Elly," he managed to say. He looked her over. She looked stunning in yet another on-point ensemble. She was wearing a bright green shirt with a black tank top underneath with matching green pants and another pair of loafers with what looked like golden palm trees on them. "Looks like a nice drink you have there."

She looked at her drink. "Oh, it's a mojito, love. I'll have to make you one sometime." She took another sip and smiled brightly at him. He smiled back at her.

"I've been thinking about you all day…My Elly."

Elly's eyes grew larger with surprise. "Albert, I haven't heard you say that in a very long time." Albert could see tears forming in the corners of her eyes. "I'm surprised you remember calling me that."

Albert thought about this for a minute. "It's difficult to say. After you left last night it kind of just came to me. It felt…right."

"I understand. It's slowly coming back to you. I'm just surprised how that came to you so quickly." She looked away for a moment and wiped her eyes.

"Why is it that you're crying, Elly?"

"Oh, they're happy tears, Albert. I'm just so very happy to see you again." Albert knew she meant a considerably longer amount of time than just one night.

"How long have you known me?" Albert said, looking into Elly's eyes unflinching.

She sat a minute contemplating her response. "I've known you for a very long time, Albert. Since you were just a boy."

"A boy? Then why don't I remember you?"

She looked down. Her brow furrowed and a piece of her bangs fell over her left eye. "I...don't know, love. How I wish I did. I've spent years waiting for you. I've been trying to reach you for a long time to varying degrees of success. Do you recall any of your lucid dreams? I came to you every chance I got."

Albert tried to think back to any of his dreams he had in the past. He focused his thoughts on anything that might have remained with him.

He recalled one particular dream of standing on a balcony looking out on a beautiful bay of palms surrounded by a beach with platinum white sands. How happy he felt and how he had been there with someone but then that someone became someone else. Became...a woman with fiery red hair.

*Wait*, Albert thought, *It couldn't be.* He looked at Elly and her dark eyes were looking at him just as he had recalled in his mind's eye. "That was you! You were there in my dream with Yvonne!"

Elly grinned slyly as she had in the dream. "Yes, that was me. I tried to kick that cunt out of your mind…but you kept obsessing over her until she hurt you. I hated seeing you obsessing over all those girls. She was never meant for you, love. None of them were. I've been with you through all the heartache and pain brought on by each of them and I've been trying my damnedest to reach you. Finally, somehow, after all this time we're together again."

Albert sat there contemplating the knowledge that Elly had been there this entire time. He felt terrible that he had wasted so much of his time on those other girls. He'd wasted so many feelings on them. He'd always had a curious feeling that *The One* was out there somewhere. He just never realized he'd already met her. As he sat there soaking all of this in, other bits and pieces of dreams came flooding back into his mind where he'd dreamed of a red-haired woman and the realization that it was Elly the entire time blew his mind.

"Maybe we should stop, for now, love. I know this is quite a lot again for you to think about."

Albert began to feel tears forming in his eyes. The thought that he'd hurt Elly weighed heavy on his heart. "I'm so sorry for wasting my time with those other girls, My Elly. With every one of them, I was searching for something I felt I'd once had before, but felt it must have only been a dream. I now know that it wasn't a dream! You're not a dream…at least not in that sense. You're my dream girl. The one I'd been searching for during all those years of misplaced love."

Elly shook her head. "Don't you apologize for anything, love. You didn't know. It's not like you did it intentionally."

Whether he did it intentionally or not. The thought still weighed on him. "I promise you, My Elly, I'll never hurt you again," he said as tears began streaming down his face.

"Oh, Albert. How I wish I could wipe those tears off of your face. I know you'll never hurt me."

Elly looked up at the dimming sky above. The light in the garden was turning that familiar hue of light pink. "Love, it's late. I think we both need some rest. It's going to be night here soon. I have an idea. How about we fall asleep together tonight!"

Albert lit up with the idea. "That sounds amazing to me. Let's do it." Elly smiled brightly at him and hopped up from her seat at the garden table. She took off toward a door leading into the large palatial estate surrounding the garden.

Albert watched as she entered the door then turned around and beckoned him to follow. He was unsure of how to do that. He imagined her lying down in bed wearing a silky night robe with her name on it. He closed his eyes for a second thinking about this and when he opened them what he saw was just that. Elly was lying on a large bed fitted with silky sheets and wearing a black silk robe with 'ELLY' adorning it. On both sides of her name were two golden palm trees similar to the ones on her loafers.

"Ready for bed, love?"

"Yes, I'm ready, My Elly," he eagerly replied, lying down.

She smiled brightly and lay her head upon one of the soft red velvet pillows. Albert put his arms behind his head so he could see Elly from across the room. "You feel so far away, love."

"You want me to move the television closer?"

"No...you'd still feel far away. That's OK though. We'll be closer soon. Like we were before..."

"Before?" Albert said, curiously.

"...Yes, love. Let's sleep now. We'll discuss that when the time is right." Albert didn't feel like pressing the matter. His eyes were already getting heavy. "Goodnight, love," was the last thing he heard before he slowly drifted off to sleep.

The next few weeks saw Albert meeting up with Elly each night in much the same way as before. He would eagerly await her arrival as the television sets darkened picture would miraculously light up and Elly would fade into focus, each time wearing another on-point ensemble.

During this time Albert began to see more and more parts of the palatial palace as each night Elly would be in a different location. Sometimes she would be in the palace itself and other times upon the platinum sands of the beach just outside its walls. Each night began to end the same within the sprawling master bedroom upon the king-size bed with its red silk sheets.

They would spend hours each night talking to one another growing ever closer. The main issue though that neither of them could figure out was why exactly they had been separated for all those years. Every time Albert thought back to his childhood it was all a big blank to him no matter how hard he thought. It was as if there was a veil in his mind preventing him from seeing the truth behind it.

Albert questioned Elly on what she could recall from those early days but she would tell him that she would discuss it with him soon…in person. Albert was told to have patience and that they would be together face to face again when the time was right. Truthfully, Albert was happy to just have her back in his life. They may very well have been separated by an immeasurable distance but Albert felt she was with him always.

Albert quickly adopted a new outlook on life. He no longer felt like lying in bed hopelessly staring up at the ceiling listening to the world pass him by outside. He got out of bed each morning with a purpose. Elly filled his life with meaning and each night little by little he felt bits of his past coming back to him.

Mid February came and one night, during one of his deep conversations with Elly, Albert recalled a little black sketchbook that his father had given to him during the last Christmas that they spent together. He was taken aback by this memory. It was as if the veil slightly rippled revealing one glimmer of a memory that he had forgotten. This memory came to him as they were discussing things that Albert used to do.

He would make random sketches in a little black sketchbook when he was young. He hadn't thought of that book in years. How could he have forgotten about such a precious thing? With this memory came even further questions, but no matter how he thought about it that veil wasn't about to ripple again.

The following morning after Albert's revelation he awoke early and looked throughout his closet for that little black sketchbook. His closet quickly bore no results and he knew the rest of his room only contained his reading desk and one empty drawer and two bookshelves full of his collection of various novels and short story collections. He thought about where else the sketchbook could have gotten to and one room sprang to his mind - his mother's bedroom.

Albert quickly walked out of his room and looked out of the diamond-shaped window upon the front door. His mother hadn't returned from work just yet. Albert remembered there had been freezing rain the night before and she must be taking her time driving back on the icy roads. He was glad for the fortuitous forecast. It meant he had time to check her room before she got home.

He ran for her bedroom which was located past the kitchen and their little laundry nook. He grasped the cold metallic doorknob and looked down at it. His reflection stared back at him as he slowly turned it. He had a bit of a manic appearance. His eyes were wide open, hair still uncombed and stubble growing upon his face.

He entered her darkened bedroom and flicked the switch for the ceiling fan on. The light was cast upon every inch of the room. Albert's eyes shifted left to right. *Where to look first?* He decided he'd skip her drawers. Nothing there but pants, shirts, and his mother's…unmentionables, which he had no desire to look at let alone rifle through. His focus fell upon her closet. *That HAS to be where it is.* Albert made his decision. That was where he was going to look.

The floorboards creaked beneath his feet as he stepped across the gray carpeting. He opened the closet door slowly and saw all of his mother's Sunday dresses hung up neatly upon the rack and some of her work scrubs.

Beneath these were six plastic multicolored containers stacked three by three. Albert grabbed the hot pink tub on the top right and set it upon the floor. He opened it to find nothing but an assortment of various t-shirts. He returned the plastic lid to the container and tried the following tub beneath it. Each container bore nothing out of the ordinary.

It was only upon Albert removing the last container that he discovered something quite curious within it. Within this container was a briefcase locked with a four number code. He shook the suitcase around and could hear various items moving about inside. He took the briefcase over to his mother's bed and set it down.

He returned the plastic containers to the closet carefully arranging them how they had been before then returned to the briefcase. He eyeballed the letters trying to think what the code could be. He noticed the initials 'D.O.' carved very small in the top right corner of the case. D.O.? Don Oden? Dad? Albert realized that this must have been his father's old briefcase.

Now that he thought of it he could vaguely recall his father coming home from business trips in his sharp suit carrying this case with him. His father had worked at a local law firm as one of its star lawyers. He could recall this but he didn't recall him inputting the code.

Albert thought he'd try a few options. Considering it was his dad's briefcase his mother's birthday might be the password. He inputted, '1027'. He then tried to open the latches, but they still wouldn't budge. He decided to try his birthday next. He input, '0607'. He felt good about this one. He tried flipping the latches open, but they stayed stubbornly locked firmly in place.

He began to rack his brain some more on what the code could be when he heard the familiar sound of his mother's Skylark slowly pulling up into the driveway outside of his mother's bedroom window. "Damn, what's the code!" Albert said to himself. He heard the motor from the Skylark shut off and imagined his mother beginning to make her way out of the car. It's now or never, he thought and decided to try one last date that sprang immediately to his mind. He input '0521', his parent's anniversary. This time the latches sprung open. Albert's mouth dropped open in amazement.

He opened the briefcase and looked over its contents hidden away for God only knew how many years. There wasn't much inside, but what was there Albert was astonished to see. On top was an old VHS tape with a white label on it. Written upon the label was one lone word in what he recognized as his mother's handwriting, *'Paradise'*. Albert moved the curious tape aside to see old photographs of Albert and his father beneath it. One of which was of Albert and his father by the Christmas tree looking at Al the Alligator.

He wished he had more time to look through the photographs but he then heard the slam of the car door outside. *Not much time left!* He lifted the old photographs and was amazed to see what he had been searching for. A small black leather-bound sketchbook cracked with age sat at the very bottom of the case. He stood for a moment in complete shock that it actually existed.

He could hear his mother's footsteps and quickly grabbed the sketchbook along with the photo of him and his father by the Christmas tree and slid it into the inside of the sketchbook. He closed the briefcase again locking the latches in place and returned it to the plastic container from whence it had come and hauled ass out of there just as his mother opened the front door.

"Good morning, Alby! The roads were so icy out there this morning I had to take my time getting home. You weren't worried were you?" Albert's mother began to slip out of her bulky black winter coat.

He turned away from her when he realized he had the sketchbook in his hands. He quickly looked for a place to hide it. *I would decide to put on a bloody pair of pajama pants without pockets today of all days*, he thought to himself when he realized pockets weren't an option. His mother turned around and smiled at him. He put his hands behind his back and opened the back of his pajama pants and slid the sketchbook down between his boxers and pants keeping it in place in the waistband. "Do you have something behind your back for me?" she asked.

Albert grinned back at her. "Yes, Ma...My arms and they're ready to hug you. I *WAS* worried. I'm glad you're home safe." Albert embraced his mother tightly and convincingly. Truth be told he had been a little worried but not enough to hug her like this.

"Oh, Alby, I'm fine. It makes me happy to know you're glad I'm home safe. Hey, would you like a bit of breakfast? I'm hungry."

Albert could feel the sketchbook beginning to slip slowly out of the grip of his waistband. "Sure, Ma. I'll be right out in a few minutes. I'm gonna comb my hair real quick."

"OK, Alby, don't forget to take your vitamin."

"Sure, Ma," he said, slowly making his way up the hallway to the bathroom.

He closed and locked the door to the bathroom right as the sketchbook slipped entirely out of the grip of his waistband. He reached down and picked the book up off of the brown tiled floor. Albert took it over to the sink and removed the elastic band keeping it held firmly closed. Upon the first page of the book were two signatures and dates written one on top of the other. The oldest on top read, 'Donald Oden - December 25, 1956' and the name below it read 'Albert Oden - December 25, 1982'.

Albert was amazed. This *WAS* the little black sketchbook he had received from his father that fateful Christmas morning. He flipped through the subsequent pages looking at faded sketches of various kinds of things from trees, to animals, to people. As the sketches progressed they became signed with 'D.O.' and progressively became more detailed and skillful. Albert kept flipping through the pages until his father's sketches stopped and several pages of scribbles took over, each signed with an atrocious scrawl, 'Albert'.

*This was where he handed the book off to me to pick up where he left off. Passing the torch as it were,* he thought to himself as he looked over his childish drawings. Albert noticed that his scribbles began to take more shape after a few pages. On one of the pages, he swore he could make out a drawing of three trees that looked quite like palm trees. He thought he could pick out three palms by a body of water with the sun in the sky. That's what he thought he saw in this childish sketch. This thought stayed in his mind and was one he couldn't shake.

He flipped the page and discovered that was the final sketch inside of the book. What followed after were many blank pages left unused. Just as he was about to close the book something caught his eye though. Upon closer inspection, Albert could make out the remnants of a page, after the three palms sketch, that had been torn out. *Why the hell would a page be missing?* He pondered as his mother came knocking upon the bathroom door. "You alright in there, Alby?"

He quickly closed the sketchbook and hid it inside of his waistband once more. "Yeah, Ma. Just had to go to the restroom." He flushed the toilet and sprayed some air freshener to make it convincing.

"OK, dear. Breakfast is ready. Come on out and eat." Albert stood there a minute longer turning the water of the sink on to "wash" his hands. He stood there looking into the mirror. *Why the hell would she hide this from me all these years? What's up with that missing page?* Albert sighed. He was presented with more questions and fewer answers. *I gotta talk to Elly about this tonight...maybe she'll know something.* Albert turned the water off in the sink and quickly ran to his room. He took the sketchbook out of his pants. He removed the photo of him and his father and stared at it a moment. A smile began to break across his face as he noticed how happy he was looking at Al inside of his light pink seashell. The light within it made him think of sunset upon that beach with Elly. "Food's ready, Alby! Come on out now!" his mother yelled from the kitchen. He quickly placed the sketchbook inside of his reading desk's drawer for safekeeping and made his way out to the table and ate his breakfast all the while mulling over all the questions he had been presented this morning.

After Albert finished his breakfast he walked back to his room and locked the door behind him. He sat down to his reading desk and opened the drawer. He reached inside and plucked the sketchbook out and opened it once more. He sat there a few minutes looking over each page meticulously. He hoped that maybe a fragment of a memory or something more would come back to him. Sadly for him, it did not.

He examined the final page that had been torn out. He ran the tips of his fingers over the remnants of paper left behind and then he noticed something. On the page that was behind the one torn out lay fine lines he could vaguely see. It appeared that when he had been drawing whatever was on that torn page that he had been pressing hard enough for it to leave traces upon the next page. He recalled a technique he had once read about in one of his novels where a detective used a pencil upon a notepad by the phone at a crime scene to discover a hastily written note revealing an important clue left behind by the perp. The clue that the detective discovered ultimately lead to the apprehension of the suspect in the end. With this knowledge in mind, Albert opened his drawer and removed an old number 2 pencil he hadn't used since his high school days a few years prior. He took the pencil to his lips and lightly kissed it. *Here's hoping this works.*

He took the pencil and turned it on its side and lightly began to move it up and down slowly across the paper. A moment later he could make out a figure of what was upon that torn out page. Although some of the finer details were missing he could make out the shape of a person's face. He felt it was a young girl but the facial features weren't present.

He sat there a moment staring at the imprint when he felt the need to erase the markings over the face. Once he removed the markings he took the pencil and began to draw eyebrows onto the featureless face. Albert hadn't drawn anything to his knowledge since these drawings in the sketchbook, yet he took the pencil and worked it effortlessly. It was like it was all coming back to him. He drew the features of the clearest face he imagined in his mind.

When he finished he sat back and looked upon the drawing again. He had drawn Elly's eyes, nose, and mouth and upon seeing the whole picture a flash of a memory came back to him. In this quick memory, he saw a young Elly sat upon the beach smiling widely with three palms behind her. The sun hung low in the sky. This memory, no matter how brief, filled him with immense happiness. They *had* been together back then. He felt that the time was coming where they would be there on that beach smiling together again.

Albert sat there for a while staring at the eyes of the drawing and trying to imagine being back there on that beach but nothing more came to him. He stood up and stretched a moment letting out a deep sigh. *I can't wait for tonight. It's going to be an interesting evening I feel*, he thought to himself, a slight smile forming upon his face.

He looked around his room drenched in gloom. He thought it felt rather depressing in here so he decided to walk over and open his drapes and let some sunshine in. He walked over to the window located over the foot of his bed and then he stubbed one of his big toes upon something large and solid underneath his bed. "Hells bells that hurt!" he lightly cursed falling onto his bed.

He rubbed his toe lightly, trying to dull the pain. After a few minutes, it subsided and he began to wonder what he had come across under his bed. *I don't recall putting anything under there.* He arose and hopped off at the foot of the bed.

He crouched down and reached underneath and grabbed what felt like a hefty tome. A moment later it all came back to him what he had placed there. *The encyclopedia! I completely forgot I still had this thing!* It's true that before he set off that morning before the debacle of his last trip to the library he had forgotten to pack up the hefty encyclopedia. In doing so it was spared the ultimate fate the other books had received. He wondered how long would it have stayed down there if he hadn't stubbed his toe on it.

He took the encyclopedia over to his desk and put it down with a light thud then returned to his window, This time without the debilitating stubbing of his toe, and opened the drapes washing his room with the bright glow of mid-day sunlight. He sat a moment in the warm rays magnified by the glass of his bedroom window then returned to the encyclopedia.

He flipped it open glancing over the numerous pages of various topics that were of no interest to him. He continued to flip through the pages until he came across one earmarked. The earmark was left by him years before when Albert was in his early teens.

He had discovered this encyclopedia while wandering through the reference book section of the library. He had chosen the book on a whim in hopes that maybe it contained some excitingly tantalizing photos within of the fairer sex. He had come across one page containing such an image. Albert found himself returning to that encyclopedia every so often and gazing upon the page containing a detailed anatomical drawing of a nude woman.

Just as he had done all of those times prior he found himself again staring at that page. The nude woman stood there completely exposed to Albert's suggestive gaze. He found his heart began to race and his mouth became dry. The excitement within him grew but he didn't know what all of this meant. Every time he had looked at this woman he grew to feel this way inside. He felt an overwhelming sense of wanting to touch her, kiss her. His desires were always left unfulfilled though. He slammed the cover shut and took some deep breaths. He looked out of his window at the deep blue cloudless sky above and closed his drapes once more.

That night Albert took his seat in front of his television set and eagerly awaited Elly's arrival. He watched the seconds tick by agonizingly slowly on his watch. Finally, the screen slowly began to illuminate with its usual static at first then the picture began to grow clearer and sharper with each passing moment. Elly came into focus upon the balcony Albert had grown quite familiar with in these subsequent weeks. "Hello, love," she said, smiling brightly at him.

"Hello, My Elly," he replied with an equally bright smile in return. "I've been desperate to talk to you all day," Albert said, reaching into his desk drawer and pulling out the little black sketchbook. Albert proceeded to share the details of the day's events with her. She sat there listening intently to Albert. The breeze from the bay lightly blew her hair partially over her eye. He opened the sketchbook and shared the images within. Elly was especially intrigued by the sketches of the three palms and herself.

She turned away from Albert looking out to the sun setting on the horizon. Her brow was furrowed. "Love, I think it's time that we come together face to face."

Albert dropped his sketchbook and was taken aback by her unexpected statement. "R-Really? When? Tonight? Let's do it!" he said, standing up.

"Hold on, Albert. I don't want to rush this. If you come here I want you to be prepared and tell your mom about your plans to leave. She'll worry about you for sure if you just disappear."

Albert sat down again and agreed, she was absolutely correct. "OK, I'll tell her tomorrow. We'll go out and have supper together and I'll explain everything to her."

"That will be great, love. Before you come you can introduce me to her. It's been a long time coming."

Albert laughed, "Yes, she always wanted to be the first one to meet my girlfriend."

"I'm your girlfriend am I?" Elly said, grinning.

Albert blushed brightly. "Well…yeah," he said looking down.

Elly giggled and smiled, "I can't wait for tomorrow."

She stood up and leaned against the balcony looking at Albert. "Was there anything else you did today, Albert?"

Albert had told her about everything he had done except for one thing. "Um, what do you mean?"

Her dark eyes pierced right through him. "Love, you can tell me," she said, continuing to stare at him. He thought she was looking past him though at his bed.

He looked over at his bed. The bulky encyclopedia was peaking out slightly. He sighed. "I can't keep anything from you, Elly. I'm sorry. I forgot I still had that encyclopedia here and I just…"

"You just wanted to see that drawing again. Oh, Albert. If you wanted to see something like that all you had to do was simply ask," Elly interjected and slowly slipped her bright red blazer off of her shoulders and tossed it upon the seat. Albert continued to watch wondering at first what she was doing. She took her loafers off next and then her bright red socks. She then slipped her belt off and unbuttoned her black shirt. Albert covered his eyes when he caught a glimpse of her black bra underneath.

He could still hear her slipping out of the rest of her clothes but he didn't dare look. It was a practice instilled in him from a young age of watching movies with his mother. Every time a raunchy scene would come upon the screen she told him to cover his eyes until it was over.

"Albert, look at me," Elly said. Her voice was soft and velvety. It was pure sex in his ears.

"I-I can't. I want to be a gentleman."

"Oh, love. It's OK. I want you to look at me…please." The way she said please was almost too much for Albert to handle. He removed his hands but kept his eyes closed. "Please, Albert. Open your eyes." He slowly opened his eyes and saw Elly standing before him. He was awestruck at how beautiful she was. She was a living breathing piece of art. Her porcelain skin glowed in the early evening moonlight. It looked so soft and smooth. He wanted so badly to touch her, caress her, pull her close to him, and kiss her deeply. "Tomorrow, love," she said to him. All Albert could do was shake his head in agreement. Elly smiled at him, "Let's try to get some rest, love." She began to walk towards the bedroom door. Albert continued to watch her in amazement as she walked away. She looked over her shoulder with a cheeky grin on her face.

Albert got up and got into bed. He looked at the screen and saw that Elly had slipped into her black velvet robe. She lay back in bed and looked longingly at Albert. "Love, I'll meet you tomorrow night at eight…this time we'll meet somewhere I haven't been in a long time."

"Where's that?" Albert asked.

"The three palms, love…our special place." Albert wanted to ask her about them but he figured he would just wait to see them for himself the following evening.

"OK, My Elly. Wait for me there. Until tomorrow night."

"Until tomorrow night, love," Elly replied. Albert didn't think he could sleep after everything that had happened but Elly always made him feel at ease. They both drifted off looking into each other's eyes growing heavier and heavier.

# Chapter 3
# Beyond The Veil

Early the next morning Albert woke to the sound of a booming voice coming from the living room. His eyes slowly opened to see the early rays of sunlight peeking through the side of his drapes, lightly illuminating his bedroom. The television set was pitch black as if everything that had occurred the night before was but a dream. Albert knew better than this though. His thoughts of questioning the validity of everything to do with Elly had ceased weeks prior. He knew he'd be seeing her face to face that evening and the thought of it made him spring from his bed with the swiftness of a child on Christmas morning.

He approached his door and listened more closely to the voice coming from down the hallway. Upon further investigation, he recognized not one but two voices conversing. He recognized the voices and slowly opened his door to find Sydney and his mother talking at the entrance of the hallway. Sydney turned to look at Albert, his face was light pink. Albert didn't know if it was from the bitter cold outside or a night's worth of drinking. Albert bet that it was a combination of the two. "Yo, Al! Just the man I came to see!" Sydney boomed.

Albert could tell he had had a drink or ten. "Good morning to you too, Syd."

"Oi, don't be cold, Al, my main man. I know it's a bit early, but I was in the neighborhood…out for an early morning walk and decided to pop in for a visit on you and your mom." Albert stood there a moment then invited Sydney to come into his room.

"Enjoy your visit, Sydney," Albert's mom said from the kitchen. "I'll tell you what. I'll bring you and Albert some hot cocoa. How does that sound?"

"Sounds great, Aunt Milly," Sydney beamed. He slid his shoes off at the door and scurried up the hallway. Albert closed the door behind him.

Sydney took a seat at Albert's reading desk and gazed at the television set. "How's the TV working out for ya, Al?" he said, looking at his reflection in the glass tube then giving it a knock with one of his knuckles.

"Don't…do that. It's been working out great, Syd. I really appreciate you giving it to me," Albert said, taking a seat at the foot of his bed.

"That's awesome. I'm glad. I was a bit worried though…" He trailed off.

"Why's that?" Albert asked wondering if maybe Sydney had experienced some similar occurrences he had been going through.

"Oh…it's just that it stopped turning on for me. I actually gave it to you because I thought you could fix it. I guess I was right. I knew you read a lot of books and were smart."

Albert hung his head and rolled his eyes. *Typical*, he thought to himself, *It's no surprise he didn't experience anything like that.* "Yeah, Syd. I fixed her right up. It was a bad vacuum tube…"

"You see! I knew you were the right man for the job! You're goddamn amazing!" Albert rolled his eyes at this remark.

Sydney turned away from Albert and looked down at the floor. He furrowed his brow and reached down below Albert's desk. "Hey, Al…looks like you dropped something here. What is this? Looks like an old photo. Hey, isn't that your dad?" Albert leaped from the foot of his bed and plucked the photograph from Sydney's fingers. "Hey, Al! What's that about! I was doing you a favor!"

Albert held the photo pressed into his chest for a moment and seeing the look of surprise upon Sydney's face felt slightly embarrassed. "Right…I apologize, Syd. This photo is just very special to me." He handed the photo back to Sydney letting him look at it again.

Sydney sat in silence for a moment staring at the photograph. "This is a nice photo. You look a lot like your old man, you know? I miss him sometimes." Sydney placed the photo upon Albert's desk and looked at his reflection in the television set.

"Al, there's another reason I came over this morning...I was at The Sexothèque until closing last night...or should I say early this morning? Anyway, they're having a special tonight for Valentine's Day. Bring a friend and you and your friend get a free lap dance. I wanted to invite you out tonight."

Albert scoffed at Sydney's invitation. "You're insatiable, you know that? What about Victoria? It's Valentine's Day! How are you going to explain that to her?"

Sydney slowly turned around with a grin. "Insatiable? Nice. Word of the day I reckon. I already have things sorted with Victoria. I told her I had to work late and that I'd be too tired to take her out later. I said we'd go out tomorrow night. She's gonna go spend the night with some friends in King City. So, do you want in or not?"

Albert looked at Sydney amazed and replied, "I'm going to have to gracefully decline your offer. I have plans of my own for tonight."

"What do you have planned for tonight, bro? I know that you and Yvonne didn't work out. If you had you wouldn't be holed up in this house day and night."

Albert turned away from Sydney and reached over to open his drapes. He moved them aside letting the early morning light stream into his room and then began looking out at the neighboring houses. "Well, no...Things between us didn't work out. That's perfectly fine with me though because I met someone else...or rather reconnected with someone." Albert began to smile. Being able to discuss Elly made him unable to contain his joy.

"Holy shit! I had no idea. Who is she? An old girlfriend from school? Details, Al. I need details!" Albert turned around to find Sydney on the edge of his seat...literally.

"Calm down there, Syd. We didn't go to school together but I've known her for a very long time. I'm...going to go be with her tonight."

Unbeknownst to Albert at this time, his mother was outside of his door holding onto two steaming mugs of hot cocoa. She had walked up around the time Syd made his gracious offer to attend The Sexothèque that night. She stood in the darkened hallway outside of Albert's door curiously listening and was about to knock on the door when Albert spoke up about his plans for that night. She then listened in further. "I'm going somewhere warm where it's just the two of us."

A devious smile formed upon Sydney's face. "Somewhere warm, eh? Oh, I bet you are. I'm going to miss you tonight, but I'm just happy that you're getting out there. It's about damn time."

Albert smiled brightly. "Yes, I agree. I've been waiting for this moment for all my life."

Sydney stood up and walked towards the door, then leaned his shoulder against it. "So, what's her name?"

Albert stuck his chest out a bit and proudly answered, "Her name is Elly."

Albert's mother, still standing in the shadows of the hallway, nearly dropped the mugs of cocoa onto the carpet below when Albert spoke that name. Her worst fear had come to pass. She walked up the hallway and into the kitchen and poured the coco down the sink then laid the mugs aside to be washed. She kept herself as collected as she could for she knew what she must do that day. It was something she hadn't done in a very long time but she had seen the signs for months now. She didn't want to believe it but when Albert spoke the name 'Elly' she knew then what must be done.

Sydney left shortly after, staggering out over the front steps onto the lawn. He had forgotten to tie his shoelaces. Albert had seen him out. Both of them were a little disappointed at not having a piping hot cup of cocoa. Albert was surprised his mother hadn't poked her head into his room while he and Sydney had been talking but he felt there was a first time for everything.

After Albert closed the front door he watched as Sydney walked off down the sidewalk and disappeared behind a large row of hedges. He turned around to find the house silent. He went to his mother's room and knocked on her door. No answer. He thought he could hear her muffled voice though. Maybe she was on the phone in her bathroom? Albert wanted to ask her about going out later that afternoon for supper. They had a good bit to discuss before his trip that night and he wanted to lay everything out for her and have her understand what his plans were.

He returned to his room and decided in the meantime he was going to begin sorting out his suitcase for his trip. He dragged an old black roller suitcase out from the back of his closet. It was covered in dust. He hadn't used this bag since he and his mother took a vacation to the mountains a few years prior. Albert recalled the beauty of the snow-covered peaks and rolling hills. He had longed to return someday but they never could find the time to go back...or rather his mother couldn't.

Albert blew a layer of dust off of the top of the bag and unzipped it. He then began to eyeball his wardrobe. He wanted to pack light, summer clothes. He found a few pairs of pastel-colored shorts tucked into the back of his wardrobe that he hadn't worn in a while. He took the teal, salmon, and lime-colored shorts, folded them, and placed them into his suitcase.

He followed the shorts with several button-up shirts and then he came across a nice juniper green double-breasted jacket he thought Elly would appreciate that he had received as a Christmas gift a few years prior from his aunt Lolita and uncle Harry. He decided to wear this particular jacket out for supper and placed it upon his bed. Pretty soon Albert's suitcase was packed and he returned it to the back of his closet for later. Having sorted out his bag Albert decided to jump into the shower and have a nice shave.

Before he exited his room he noticed the photograph that Sydney had lain upon his desk. He picked it up and stared at it for a few moments. A melancholic feeling struck him while looking at his father. Did he look like him? He hadn't thought about it. *Now's not the time for this*, he thought and opened the drawer of his desk, and grabbed the sketchbook and slid the photo into the middle of its pages for safekeeping.

He turned around and then fetched his bag from his closet and placed the sketchbook inside of it. He wanted to replace the torn drawing he had created of Elly with a new one. That was one of many things he decided he would do when he got there that night.

He went into his bathroom and got undressed lying his clothes in a neatly folded pile on top of the toilet. He stepped into the shower and adjusted the water to his liking. He then turned on his shower radio and found a nice song being played on this light AM station and began to lather his hair up. He quickly found himself dancing and snapping his fingers to the beat. He almost slipped and decided to stick to just the finger-snapping. He certainly was in a great mood.

After his dance number was complete he stepped out of the shower and gave himself a close shave. He wanted to look his absolute best for Elly. He looked into the mirror still cloaked in steam and winked at himself. He was ready to see her face to face now. He could hardly contain himself.

He began to think about being with her on that beach under the three palms holding her tightly and feeling her warmth against him. He found himself becoming lost in this thought when a KNOCK KNOCK KNOCK came from outside the bathroom door. "Albert?" his mother said with a concerned tone.

Albert came flying back from his thoughts and answered flustered, "Yeah, Ma?"

She answered a few seconds later, "Let's go out for supper. How about we go out for pizza and wings at your favorite place in King City?"

Albert hadn't expected this. He had wanted to go out with her anyway, but to go out to Polo's Pizza was usually reserved for birthdays. "Sure, Ma. I'd love to go to Polo's."

"OK, Albert. Let me go and get ready. I'll come to get you in a bit." She replied rather flatly. Albert felt something was off with her but shrugged it off. *Maybe she's tired*, he thought to himself then began to get dressed and returned to his thoughts of caressing Elly.

Albert returned to his room, got dressed and laid out on his bed still entranced in his thoughts of what all he was going to do with Elly that night. He waited for his mother but didn't mind her taking her time. He had plenty to think about in the meantime with not only Elly but how to tell his mother about her. After a while, a knock came upon Albert's door. "Come in!" Albert said, happily.

His mother opened the door slowly. She didn't come in but simply said from the doorway, "Let's go, Albert." She then turned away and walked out the front door. *She has an awfully somber look on her face. It's like we're going to a funeral or something. She really must be worn out from work. Supper will be great though. We'll have some laughs and she always enjoys going out together.*

Albert got up from his bed and before he walked out of his room he placed his hand on top of his television set. "I'll be there soon, My Elly," he said in the silence of his room. He closed his door and then walked outside finding his mother already in the car, engine running.

He walked out to the car and the cold February wind began to cut through him like a knife. He pulled his juniper green double-breasted jacket closed and ran for the Skylark. Maybe he should have chosen a heavier jacket but it was too late now. He just figured he would get dressed for the night early.

He hopped into the warm inviting back seat and everything was alright then. He buckled up and his mother backed out of their driveway onto the road and they were off. Albert was looking forward to the pizza and wings. He sat there a moment waiting for his mother to start chiming in with something about Sydney stopping by or ask what Sydney had wanted but she kept driving not saying a word. He decided to let her drive and began to look out of the window onto the passing scenery of Lando. He began thinking back to Elly again and thought they'd be there in no time if he just slipped back into his thoughts.

After a little while, Albert began to notice something strange. He had tried to slip back into his thoughts but he had a sensation come over him that something was wrong. His mother had taken a road he'd not expected her too. She was on a back road instead of the highway which was the much faster route to King City.

Albert felt a strange sense of déjà vu come over him as he looked out upon the passing trees and fields. They passed a large pond with a dock built by it. In the middle of the pond was a large weeping willow on a tiny island. It's branches covered the tiny island in a thick shade. As Albert sat there staring at this tree a memory began to come back to him. This time it wasn't just a snippet but a full-blown series of events. He shut his eyes and thought back…

He felt the warmth of the sun basking over him. There were three palm trees above him. He was lying there on a towel. He wasn't alone though. A young girl with long fiery red hair lay facing towards him. She was sleeping. Albert faced her and put his arm around her. Her dark brown eyes slowly opened and she began to smile at him. They lie there for what could have been hours looking into each other's eyes when Albert sat up. "Elly, I remembered that I left my sketchbook back home. I want to draw."

"OK, love. Let's go get it." The two of them walked to the tall grass to a cliff-side. Within the cliff-side lie a cave.

"I wish you could come with me, Elly."

"Me too, love. I'll be right here waiting for you though." Albert entered the cave to find a small wooden door at the back. He grabbed the handle and opened it. Albert crawled out onto his closet floor. He closed the crawl space door behind him and quickly set about to grab his sketchbook. He grabbed it off of his small bookshelf but before returning through the doorway again he decided to see what his mother was doing.

He slowly opened the door to his room and could hear her in the living room. She was crying. *She's done that a lot lately...ever since Daddy...*, his thought trailed off. He didn't want to think about his father right now. He turned around and walked back to his room. When he was right outside the door a loud creak came up from the floorboards.

"Albert? Albert is that you?!" He didn't want to see his mother right now. Not with tears rolling down her face. "Albert?!" He could hear her walking towards the hall. He quickly closed his door and ran back into his closet flinging the crawl space door open.

He entered the cool cave and heard his mother calling to him one last time before he closed the door behind him. He exited the cave to find Elly leaning against a tree with a bored look on her face. She looked over at him and smiled. "It's about time!" she said.

"Sorry...I got it here though." He held the sketchbook triumphantly above him. They made their way through the thick grass and sugar weeds back onto the platinum white sands of the beach.

Albert breathed a deep breath of salty sea air and noticed the sun hanging low in the sky behind the three palms in the distance. The emerald hills in the background provided a striking image that Albert couldn't pass up. This was to be his first real sketch in the book his father had given him for Christmas. "Wait…I need to draw this," he said to Elly and quickly put his pencil to paper. Elly watched over his shoulder as the scene began to take shape. Soon he completed it. "Maybe I'll go back and color it in later?"

"That would be great, love," Elly said, hugging him. "Race you to the trees!" she quickly yelled, breaking into a sprint. Albert tried catching up with her but she was way ahead of him. He found himself captured by her beauty yet again. Even though they were just children, Albert felt the purest, earliest form of attraction to her.

He made it to the three palms way behind Elly. "I beat you, slowpoke." He smiled at her. Even if he had been trying he'd have let her win any day.

"Can I draw you, Elly?" he said, holding his sketchbook close to his chest. She smiled at him. The breeze off of the bay lightly blew through her hair.

"Of course you can." She sat down on her towel and stayed still as Albert began to draw her. Sometimes he found himself pressing down a little too hard when she would look at him. He kept his composure though and continued onwards. He took great care with her features, especially her eyes.

"OK, have a look," he said, handing her the book. She looked at the drawing of herself. Below the drawing were Albert's initials and the title, 'My Elly'.

"I...I love it!" she said, jumping towards Albert and kissing him. Albert wasn't expecting this. It only lasted a second but Albert felt every cell within his body ignite.

The two of them spent the next few days together inseparable. Each day blended perfectly with the next. They spent most of their days playing on the beach and shared a cozy twin bed in their home by the sea.

Albert was a million miles away from any care in the world until he began to think of his mother. He thought of how sad she was. He wanted her to smile and be as carefree as he was.

While he and Elly sat below the three palms,(their favorite spot on the beach), Albert confessed his feelings about his mother to Elly. Elly agreed that his mother must be very sad and lonely and that she felt bad for her. "Wait for me here under the three palms, My Elly. I won't take long. You can meet my mother and we'll all be happy."

Elly agreed and hugged Albert goodbye. Before he disappeared into the tall grass he turned around to see Elly standing there looking out to sea. She was so beautiful. The wind off the bay blew her long fiery hair far behind her. He then turned around and followed the pathway to the cave.

He exited the crawl space door and closed it behind him. Upon opening his closet door he discovered the door to his room wide open. He walked over to the door and slowly walked down the hall avoiding the creaky board. He didn't hear his mother in the living room this time. There was nothing but silence.

He walked to his mother's bedroom and slowly opened the door. "Ma?" he said. His mother was lying asleep in bed. He walked over to her and tapped her shoulder. "Ma, wake up."

Her eyes slowly opened and she stared at Albert for a moment then bolted up. "Oh, my stars! Albert?! It's you! It's really you!"

Albert was surprised to hear her say this. "Yes, Ma. Who else would I be?"

She sat up on the side of her bed. "Where have you been, Albert? It's been days! Do you know that there are all kinds of people out looking for you?!"
"Ma, I've been away at this wonderful place! It's so bright and happy there. I want you to come back with me."

His mother sat there unable to understand. "Where were you, Albert?" she asked, totally perplexed.

"I was with Elly on the beach. We spent every day playing there and we have our own home by the sea!" Albert's mother began to cry again. "Ma, please don't cry. It'll all be better soon. Just follow me."

"Oh, Albert...dear, dear me. Show me where you were." Albert smiled at her, "Follow me!" He took off running for his room. His mother followed close behind. "It's in here," Albert said, pointing at the crawl space door. His mother hung her head. "Come on. Let's go! Elly's waiting for us," he said and began to open the small door.

His mother quickly spoke up, "Hey, how about we go pick up some food before we leave. We'll have a party for the three of us. Let me...go get ready first, Albert." He thought that was a great idea and waited for her to get ready. He waited patiently for her to return. After a long while, she came back with her car keys. "OK, let's go, Albert."

As they drove along Albert's mother kept passing by store after store where they could have easily bought food and supplies for the party. "Ma, you could have gone to that store. Where are we going?" She reassured him that they were going to the best store around and that they'd help with the party. Albert sat back and looked out the window. Pretty soon he stopped seeing stores and began to see nothing but trees. "This store must be pretty far," he said to her.

"Oh, yes, it's on the edge of town." He continued to look out of the window as the sun began to set on this warm early summer afternoon. He noticed a large pond with a dock and a large tree on a small island. He didn't know what kind of tree it was, but he thought it looked pretty neat.

"Are we close to the store yet?"

"Oh, yes. Just around the corner now."

Albert smiled and said, "You're going to be SO happy, Ma. No more tears." Albert noticed a tear rolling down her cheek. "Why do you cry? What's wrong?"

"These are happy tears, Alby. I'm just SO happy you're thinking of me."

"I just want you to be happy like me," Albert replied. She began to cry even more when Albert saw a large sprawling series of buildings ahead of them on the road. They passed by a sign above a large gate that read, Duke's End. "Is this the party store?" Albert asked, gleefully.

"Yes, Alby. They're expecting us. I phoned ahead." His mother pulled up to the biggest building's entrance and stopped the car. A large man in white came out of the front entrance followed by a man in a long white coat and a nurse. The large man opened Albert's door. "Come, sir. We've everything for your party inside." Albert took the man's large hand and waited for his mother.

"Aren't you coming, Ma?"

His mother stifled her crying for a moment. "I'll be in soon, Alby. I love you!" Albert went inside of this large building with the man and what lay inside wasn't party supplies.

Albert came flying back to the present. Everything after that was clear as day. He had spent months in that God awful place being told everything he had experienced with Elly was nothing more than the work of a hyperactive imagination.

He had been diagnosed with a fantasy-prone personality disorder by the doctors in charge and forced to take medication that subdued essentially everything that made Albert himself. They determined that he had made his way into the crawl space and holed up in there for days lost in a fantasy believing he was on a beach with Elly but he was only lying alone in the dark. After a while, he began to believe what they were telling him.

It had come back to him all at once in the back of the car. He sat there reeling from everything when he could see the tops of familiar buildings peeking over the horizon. A moment later the sprawling grounds of Duke's End spread out before him. "No...NO! I WON'T GO BACK!" He screamed trying to open the door but found they remained firmly locked. "YOU CAN'T DO THIS! HOW COULD YOU?!" He yelled at his mother who kept driving along closer and closer to the front entrance. They passed through the large gate again.

"You haven't been taking your vitamins, Albert. You're seeing that "girl" again. Albert...Elly doesn't exist."

Albert became furious at this. "Yes, she DOES!! She's as real as you or me! You haven't even seen her! How can you say that?!"

Albert looked at his watch. '5:38' it read. *No, no, no. I have to get back home by 8! Elly's waiting for me under the three palms! I can't leave her waiting there again!!* His mother continued driving along down the road pulling around the large ornate fountain out front and stopping the car.

"I'm sorry, Albert. I'm doing this because I love you."

Albert laughed, "Really? You could have fooled me...You've really fucked me over you know that? You have no bloody idea. I'll never forgive you for this!" She began to sob as two burly orderlies came out of the front entrance. One walked over to Albert's door the other to the opposite side. Albert climbed over the seat and tried opening the front passenger door but the orderly grabbed him when he climbed over. He pulled Albert out of the car and had him firmly in his grip. Albert tried squirming away but to no avail.

"Alright. Alright. We can do this one of two ways. You can go quietly or you can go kicking and screaming."

With no hesitation, Albert screamed at the top of his lungs, "KICKING AND SCREAMING, PLEASE!!" The burly orderlies each took one arm as Albert did just that. To anyone watching it looked as if Albert was a raving lunatic.

A few minutes later the orderlies arrived with Albert in tow outside of a padded room. Albert continued to resist the pulls of the two men but was cast onto the soft bed that lies in the back corner. Moments later a figure appeared behind the two men.

"Good evening, Mr. Oden. My what a ruckus you've created. You did the same thing the last time you were here, my dear boy." An older man stood in the doorway wearing a long white coat. On the chest of his coat was a name badge. 'Dr. Collins' it read.

"Do you remember me, Albert?" The good doctor inquired.

Albert stared intensely at the man. He remembered him. He remembered everything. Back when he was a kid Dr. Collins had a bit more hair though. His dome had a bright gleam to it now. "Yes, I remember you," Albert spoke.

"Ah, that's good. I was afraid you'd possibly forgotten me after all these years. We certainly didn't expect to see you back again. Don't worry. You shouldn't be here too long…as long as you're cooperative with us." Albert sat upon the edge of the bed. He hung his head down looking at the padded floor beneath him. He couldn't believe he was back in one of these rooms yet again. *They honestly think I'm crazy*, he thought.

Albert looked over at Dr. Collins's shadow upon the floor. It disappeared for a moment then reappeared. The orderlies were still across from Albert eyeballing him and ready to grab him if he tried to make a run for it. "OK, Albert. I have a little something here that will help you sleep."

Albert looked up and saw the good doctor holding a large needle in his left hand full of something Albert wanted no part of. He jumped up onto the bed and against the wall. "No. I don't need that stuff to sleep. I'll be alright." Albert spoke as calmly as he could.

Dr. Collins shook his head. The gleam from the light in the hallway bouncing off of it caught Albert's eye. "That won't do. Trust me this will help you sleep and keep those bad thoughts away all at once."

Albert thought about this statement for a moment. *Bad thoughts? What bad thoughts did he mean? Wait...could he mean Elly?* Albert's eyes grew wide. This was a horrifying thought. They aimed to take Elly away from him again. Just as they had done before. Dr. Collins grew closer and Albert gave the good doctor a swift kick across his chrome dome sending him reeling back into the adjacent wall.

He dropped the needle and Albert leaped for the door. One of the burly orderlies caught him mid-air though and as swiftly as he had jumped from the bed he was on it again. This time though he was upon his back. Both orderlies held him down. He thrashed wildly and began screaming. "NO! YOU'RE NOT TAKING MY ELLY FROM ME! NO! NO! GET AWAY! GET THE HELL OFF OF ME!!"

Dr. Collins stood up wiping a bead of sweat from his brow. He was visibly agitated. "OK, Albert, that's enough of this nonsense. You go to sleep now." Dr. Collins took the needle and one of the orderlies held onto Albert's left arm firmly. He slid the needle slowly into Albert's skin and injected him full of whatever it contained within. It was fast acting because moments later Albert felt his body grow heavy. He couldn't fight any longer. He couldn't keep his eyes open and the last thing he saw before the darkness enveloped him was the smug look on the good doctor's face and that blinding gleam upon his head.

# PART II
# DUKE'S END

# Chapter 4
# Albert Flew Over The Cuckoo's Nest

Within the darkness, Albert stood alone. The darkness was absolute around him. Within this void, he began to walk forward. As he walked he began to see a beacon of light in the far off distance. It was almost calling to him. He started walking slowly towards it then his walk became a jog. The light grew closer and more defined. He began sprinting towards this beacon of hope in front of him. Once he got close enough he recognized what it was that was casting out this light upon the dark void around him. He stopped dead in his tracks and looked into the light.

It was sort of like a window, Albert couldn't think of anything else to compare it to. He approached the "window" and looked through it. On the other side, Albert could see the platinum white sands of his beach at sunset and the three palms swaying lightly in the bays breeze.

Under the palms stood Elly. She stood with her arms folded around herself looking out upon the bay as the final rays of golden light upon the distant hills slowly faded. She turned slightly and Albert could see upon her cheek a single tear rolling downwards. Upon seeing this, the tears began to flow down his cheeks.

He yelled, "Elly, I'm right here! Turn around!" She continued to stand there, waiting for Albert. The sun had set but there wasn't any full moon out in the sky. Albert began to notice ominous clouds forming in the distance. Flashes of lightning began to splinter from them far out across the water.

The three palms began to sway faster. There was no longer a breeze coming off of the bay now but a gust. Elly still stood in place undeterred by the impending storm. Her bangs blew wildly in the wind. Albert tried to yell again, this time louder, "ELLY! TURN AROUND! IT'S DANGEROUS OUT THERE!" She still couldn't hear him.

He began to bang against the sides of the "window" in front of him. BANG! BANG! BANG! He put everything he had into trying to get her to notice him. After the third blow Elly slowly turned around. Her eyes were bloodshot and her cheeks covered in tears. Albert wanted to run to her so badly. He wanted to embrace her, to hold her tightly, and to wipe the tears away.

Albert opened his mouth to call out to her again but with a loud shatter, the "window" in front of him exploded into fragments and dissolved into nothing. Albert fell backward and landed upon his back. He stared up at the blackness. It felt all-encompassing. There was nothing around him. He felt an utter lack of hope begin to fill him and it made him feel absolutely mad. The feeling began to fill him to the point of running over and then he fell.

He wasn't sure if he was indeed falling because there was nothing but darkness around him. He just had the sensation that he was traveling at breakneck speed. He began to scream but he found his screams muffled and distorted as if they weren't coming from within him. He continued to fall for seconds, minutes, hours. He had no concept of time in this place.

He began to embrace the darkness, at least he felt a part of himself did. He fought against this and thought of something that fought off the darkness inside of him. Elly's face. He imagined every detail, every strand of hair, her eyes. The thought of her filled him with hope. He wasn't going to let that go. As he continued to fall Albert could swear that he heard someone call out to him. "Albert? Mr. Oden?" Who could be calling me? The darkness around him began to fade then and Albert found himself staring up at the face of a nurse in a blindingly white uniform.

Albert's eyes slowly adjusted to the morning light cascading into the padded room he was in. For one fleeting second, he couldn't remember where he was. It all came back to him though as it does with anyone who's just woken, especially someone woken from a nightmare such as his. "Good morning, Mr. Oden. How are you feeling this morning? Are you feeling more relaxed since last night? You gave Frank, Mort, and Dr. Collins quite a time." *Who the hell are Frank and Mort? Oh, she must mean those two neanderthals. Another question is what the hell am I wearing?* Albert looked down at the teal robe and matching pajamas he was wearing. "Are you OK, Albert?" she said to him. A genuine sound of care came from her voice.

"Yes, I'm fine," Albert muttered to her. He looked up at her and upon her too clean uniform lie her name badge which read, 'Candice'.

"Good. I'm glad to hear that. Today will be your first full day here. We want to take things slow for you. Would you like to go out for a small tour? Stretch your legs a bit?" Candice must not have been here back then. She mustn't be aware that I've already been here before. I'm well aware of what this godforsaken place looks like.

Albert forced a smile and replied, "Sure, Candice. I'd like that. One quick question though. What happened to my clothes?"

She smiled again and explained, "Oh, Mort had to fit you with the robe and such last night. It's what all the clients here wear."

Albert thought of that big ape undressing him and he failed to refrain a visible shiver. "Right...thanks, Candice."

"Of course. Are you ready for the tour?" She replied, smiling.

He stood up from the soft mattress beneath him and Candice led him out of his room onto the cool reflective linoleum floor of the hallway. Albert had failed to notice the night before the intricate pattern beneath the reflective coating of fresh wax. The previous night was nothing but a blur to him. He remembered bits and pieces. The main thing he knew was that he wanted to get the hell out of here as quickly as possible.

Candice, with great energy, began describing the current wing of Duke's End. Albert was half listening to her spiel. After Candice wrapped up the tour she returned him to his room where she said Dr. Collins would be around later to speak with him. Albert nodded his head in understanding and Candice exited the room.

Once she left Albert walked over to his window and looked out of it. Bars obscured the view slightly but he could see the inner courtyard. He saw throngs of people in teal colored robes much like the one he had been fitted with. It looked as if they were congregating out in the courtyard for some time outside or something. Some of them played basketball while others just sat around talking and some even smoked cigarettes or at least it looked that way. It was possible that it was their breath and not smoke they were exhaling in the freezing mid-February morning outside.

"Enjoy the view, Mr. Oden?" Albert quickly turned around to see Dr. Collins standing at the door. In the hallway behind him stood one of the lummoxes from the previous night, Frank. He was a mountain of a man, perfect for the job at hand. He must have stood six and a half feet tall with a blonde crew cut and black horn-rimmed glasses. He looked like Drew Carey on steroids.

Albert fixated his gaze upon the good doctor before him. "It's alright," he said, folding his arms and leaning back against the bars on the window.

Dr. Collins smiled softly. "It's good to see you've calmed down a bit, my dear boy." There's that condescending tone again. Albert was waiting for it. "You…gave us quite the time last night. I haven't seen Frank here break a sweat in a long time. Kudos, Mr. Oden."

Albert looked back at Frank who was standing there menacingly. He was waiting to spring into action if Albert were to create a ruckus once again. "When can I leave?" Albert inquired.

Dr. Collins let out a chuckle. "You've only just arrived, Mr. Oden. We've yet to even begin your treatment properly."

Albert unfolded his arms and stepped closer to Dr. Collins. "What kind of treatment do I need? I'm not crazy."

"No one said you were, dear boy. We don't like to use that word around here."

Albert rolled his eyes. "Call it what you will. I'm perfectly sane!"

Dr. Collins took the back of his hand and rubbed it against his cheek. "Do you have anything to say about this Elly nonsense?"

Albert's eyes lit up and he became angry at him calling what he and Elly shared as nonsense. "Don't you dare speak that way about Elly! Do you understand me?!" Frank took a step closer to the door to show that if Albert wanted to act up things wouldn't end well.

Dr. Collins raised his hand stopping Frank and took a step out into the hallway and replied, "Albert, you're delusional. You need some more time to cool down. I'll see you next week and we can begin your therapy."

Albert couldn't believe what he had heard. "Next week? You mean I have to stay in this padded room an entire week?!" Albert took off for the door, but Frank closed it firmly in his face and locked it tight. Albert beat upon the soft door and yelled obscenities at the good doctor and Frank calling them just about everything under the sun.

Throughout the next week, Albert sat alone in his room trying to come up with some escape plan to get back home. He didn't care how far away it was or what he had to do to get there he just had to get back there. He felt Elly was waiting for him.

He slept as much as he could in hopes that each time he'd see Elly in his dreams, but each time he fell asleep he saw nothing but the sprawling blackness from before. Pretty soon Albert could only sleep at night.

Albert began to suspect they were drugging him somehow. Maybe it was from the water Candice brought to him or the three square meals a day he received. Each time he ate he felt something inside of himself become duller. It was like an essential part of him was being clipped to not be as dangerous.

He started to set his food aside after the third day. Candace had come into his room after breakfast and asked why he had not eaten his food. Albert responded that he hadn't been very hungry. She suspected that maybe he had a bad stomach and brought him some medicine to take. He explained to her that she was very nice to have brought him some medication but he would be fine. When lunch came and he still refused to eat she asked again why he had no appetite. He simply said he wasn't hungry.

That night Mort came by to serve Albert his supper. Mort, much like Frank, was a beast of a man. Mort had a completely bald head though and tiny black eyes set in a large head. Everything was large about Mort except for his eyes.

When Mort came into his room he had handed the tray to Albert very gingerly. His hands were massive. Albert felt Mort's entire hand could eclipse his face. Mort had spoken to him, "Dr. Collins is concerned about you, sir." Albert was a bit taken aback. His voice was very soft and refined. He had expected something booming and intimidating. Mort continued, "Candace reported that you refused to eat your breakfast and lunch. Dr. Collins instructed me to serve your supper to you personally. Please, sir, you must eat."

Albert stood there a moment and realized that voice sounded so familiar. Then he remembered Mort was the man who had walked him inside all those years ago. *It's amazing but his hands are still so big even now*, Albert thought as he stared at those hands as they rested at Mort's sides.

Albert sat down on his bed and began to eat. He knew that if he refused Mort might just get Frank and the two of them might force-feed him. Anything was possible in this madhouse.

His supper consisted of warm chicken soup. *Just lovely. I really wanted to think about THAT again tonight.* Albert pushed that day in the library out of his mind and downed the bowl of soup as quickly as he could. "Don't forget your water, sir." Albert picked up the plastic cup and threw the water back in one gulp. "Thank you, sir. Have a good evening."

Mort took the tray and turned around and left. For a man of such a size, he moved very silently. That thought made Albert even more uneasy. He imagined Mort taking huge steps behind him and taking those massive hands of his and grabbing Albert by the head eclipsing all light until he was surrounded by that darkness again. Albert shook off the nightmarish thought and gazed out of his window. "I gotta get the hell outta here," he said to himself.

The remaining days saw Albert being served his meals personally by Mort. Each time Mort would stand there, his hulking frame taking up the entire width of the door. He would set his beady little eyes upon Albert and he would feel compelled to eat every last morsel of food upon his tray.

Albert found himself awoken one morning to Candace's voice. "Good morning, Albert." Albert's eyes sprung open and he looked at Candace. Her uniform still retained its whiteness. It was so clean. Almost too clean to believe. "Today we're transferring you to a real room! I know you've been waiting for that!"

Albert sat up and threw his legs over the side of his bed. He looked out of his window and could see that it was a gray and rainy day outside. "Yes, I was beginning to lose track of the days in here. It's been really boring."

She smiled brightly. Her smile was just as white as her uniform. "Excellent. Let's get you to your new room." Albert got up and began to follow her. He stepped out onto the linoleum floor again and could see his reflection slightly within it's mirrored surface. They walked through corridor after corridor.

Albert passed two young-looking guys along the way next to a door that lead outside into the courtyard. They looked over at him as he walked by. One of them smiled smugly at him, but Albert turned away before further interaction could occur. They turned another corner and Candace stopped. "Here we are, Albert. You're in Wing A now which houses a lot of younger men like yourself. I hope you can get out there and maybe speak to some of them today. Maybe introduce yourself and make some new friends?"

Albert was having none of that. He muttered a quick, "Thank you," and then tried to open his door. He found it was locked. "Um, are you sure this is the right room? The door's locked."

She frowned, "You didn't want to go into your room right now, did you? We keep client rooms locked during the day so people don't stay in bed all day. We want people to socialize, exercise, and get fresh air."

Albert hung his head for a moment. "Rules. Rules...what was I thinking," he said, displeased.

"It's OK, Albert. You can get into your room this evening. Your bed and everything you need has already been prepared." Candace looked at her watch and gasped. "I need to get back, Albert. Why don't you go out into the yard and get some air?" She bid Albert farewell and quickly turned around and went back the way they had come.

He breathed in deep and stood outside of his room a moment trying the door handle once more in hopes that by some miracle it had miraculously opened itself. No such luck. He exhaled and muttered to himself, "Fucking hell's bells."

"Whoa, there watch your mouth, buddy." Albert turned around and was greeted by two guys he saw just before. The young guy who smiled at Albert spoke again. "I heard ya, buddy. Plain as day. You might wanna ease off on the colorful language. The nurses don't take kindly to it."

Albert tried to walk past the group, but one of them threw their arm out to stop him. "Whoa, there, Panama Red, where you think you goin' to? We was talkin' to ya. You a rude one ain't ya?"

Mr. Smug spoke up again. "All we wanted to do was say hello, but one of my pet peeves is rude people. You seem to be pretty god damn rude." Albert could feel the three guys ganging up on him. *What a wonderful welcoming committee*, he thought as the two continued to run off their mouths.

"Excuse me, gentlemen. What is going on out here?" The two guys turned around and Albert looked up to see Dr. Collins. "Please disperse immediately. Go on outside or something."

The two slowly walked away but not without Mr. Smug throwing one final look over his shoulder before he went around the corner. "Looks like you're already making friends, dear boy. A word of advice...stay away from Jeremy and Leo. Jeremy is especially troublesome. He's the one who likes to smile all the time..."

Albert shook his head. "Can I get into my room, please?" Albert said, crossing his arms.

"I'm sorry, Albert, rooms are to remain locked until the evening. I do hope that you can adhere to the rules...or maybe you want to go back to your previous accommodation?"

Albert hung his head and gritted his teeth. "No, I don't."

"OK, Albert. I'll see you around then." Dr. Collins walked past Albert down the hallway then turned a few moments later to add, "Oh, yes, before I forget we have an appointment this afternoon. Meet me in my office around the corner here at 1:00."

Albert looked puzzled. "What's the appointment for?"

The good doctor responded, "My dear boy have you forgotten already? It's the start of your therapy! We'll be having a one on one therapy session. See you then, and please do remember what I said about those two." Albert was unsure of what this therapy entailed but whatever it was he wasn't looking forward to it.

Albert furrowed his brow, gave one last glance at the door to his room, then shoved his hands into the pockets of his teal sweatpants and sauntered off down the hallway towards the door Jeremy and Leo had been next to earlier. Albert turned the corner and luckily the two were no longer present. He walked up to the door and was amazed at the size of the massive inner courtyard before him. He gazed out of the large glass window alongside the door and looked out upon all of the commotion going on outside.

Dozens of men and women in teal uniforms ran, walked, and sat scattered around the yard. The gray clouds from earlier had parted halfway and allowed a few rays of sunlight to shine down upon sections of the courtyard. Albert looked over at an area to his left that no one was occupying. It was a small bench under a large pine tree. Albert decided he would venture out to that bench and get some fresh air.

He slowly put his hand upon the frigid metal of the door and immediately he second-guessed his decision once the frigid air hit him. He pressed onward though not wanting to give up so easily. He kept his eyes fixated on the bench and tried not to draw any attention toward himself. He wanted nothing to do with these people here. As far as he was concerned he was the only sane person in the entire complex.

When he reached the bench he noticed it was dry as a bone. It had been lightly raining off and on during the early morning but Albert was pleased to see that the tree's thick branches offered a cover from the rain. He took a seat upon the lightly weathered wooden bench and could feel the cold penetrate his skin even through his robe and thick sweatpants.

After a few minutes, the cold subsided and Albert leaned back and looked up into the branches of the tree. A few rays of sunlight streamed through them. One of the rays fell upon Albert's face and he could feel the soft warmth radiate upon his cheek. He exhaled a deep breath and steam came flowing out of him. *I should be on that beach right now feeling the sun on my skin…instead, I'm here in this godforsaken place with only a little sliver of light warming my cheek. My Elly…I'm so sorry.* Albert hung his head down then began to lightly sob into the teal robe around him. He felt overwhelmed and all he could think of was how long would he have to wait?

Albert dried his tears and looked up towards the entrance he had gone out of earlier. All of the people who were outside were lining up and going back inside now. He wondered what was going on but continued to sit upon the bench until a young woman walking by noticed him. She looked to be around Albert's age with blonde hair and bright blue eyes. She walked over to him. "Hi, I don't think I've seen you here before. It's lunchtime. Wanna grab a bite to eat?"

Albert looked up at her. A light breeze blew through her hair sending part of her bangs over one of her eyes. For a moment she reminded him of Elly. "Um, sure. I guess so," Albert managed to mumble.

"Great, I'm Elaine. What's yours?"

Albert laughed a moment. *God doth have a sense of humor*, he thought to himself. "Albert," he replied.

"OK, Al, let's go." Albert began to follow Elaine listening to her explain the schedule of the day. Apparently, after lunch, you could meet with visitors or place phone calls and then they had a movie they were going to play. It seemed that the schedule around here hadn't changed since he left. Everything seemed to be the same as when he was here in the past.

Everything had hit him like a ton of bricks in the car ride here. God, how he wished the veil had been moved earlier. If it had he'd be far away from here without a care in the world.

As he sat there next to Elaine in the cafeteria rambling on and on about this and that he hardly heard anything she said. It seemed like she only wanted someone to listen to her go on and on. She found a perfect match with Albert.

Albert hardly touched the pizza they had served him. If that's what you could call it. It was a square cut piece of dough with tomato sauce on it and small meaty chunks of "Pepperoni". It reminded him of the slop they tried to pass off as pizza during his school days.

After lunch ended Elaine parted ways with Albert. "Bye, Al, I gotta meet up with my folks for a bit. It was great talking to you." She tossed him a wink. Those bright blue eyes shimmering from the artificial light above.

*Yeah, great "talking" to you too,* he thought as he glanced over to the clock on the wall outside of the cafeteria. '12:55' it read. It was about time to meet up with Dr. Collins. *The joy of joys,* Albert thought as he frowned and began walking down the hallway.

The bright gleam off of the linoleum reminded him of the good doctor's dome. He averted his gaze and looked up pressing onward. After a few minutes, he arrived at a door with a sign to the right which read 'Charles Collins PsyD'. *This must be the place,* Albert thought as he grabbed the handle of the door and turned it slowly.

Albert entered the warm office and was greeted by a woman with bright red hair sitting behind a desk. She had a look of utter boredom upon her face. Albert approached the desk and began to speak, "I have an appointment with Dr. Collins for 1:00."

She frowned at him, "OK, have a seat. He'll be with you soon." Albert nodded and took a seat upon a squishy leather sofa.

A few minutes later Albert heard Dr. Collins' voice come over the intercom upon the desk. "Laura, can you send Mr. Oden in now, please?"

The woman looked down and hit a button, "Alright." Laura looked up at Albert gesturing towards the door to her left. Albert understood and walked over and entered Dr. Collins' main office.

"Good afternoon, Mr. Oden," Dr. Collins said jovially as Albert entered the room. "How has your day been so far? I do hope you made some new acquaintances and enjoyed the pizza for lunch. Please, have a seat here." He patted the back of a cushy blue quilted chair and Albert walked across the room and did as he was instructed.

"My day has been alright. I did meet someone new…a girl. Her name's Elaine." Dr. Collins took a seat across from Albert. "Oh, yes. I know her. A bit of a chatterbox that one. I do hope she let you get some words in."

Albert shook his head. "No, not really, but that's fine. I mainly just got her to show me around a bit."

"Ah, I understand. At least you managed to meet someone new though." Dr. Collins crossed his legs and began to look over a clipboard he had been carrying. "Let's jump right in now. There are some things we need to begin to discuss. For starters…" He plucked a pen from the front pocket of his white coat and began to write a few things. Albert wondered what he could be writing when he had just sat down and had barely spoken.

"…Your mother was very concerned about you. She and I have known each other for a long time now. She called me expressing great concern towards you. As she explained everything, it all sounded very similar to how things were when you were a boy…Let's discuss a few things about that." Albert leaned back in the comfortable chair trying not to roll his eyes at his mother's "great concern".

The good doctor continued, "You were brought here last time shortly after the tragic passing of your father." Albert looked away. This topic wasn't something he was comfortable hearing let alone discussing.

"Albert, I know this might not be the easiest of topics to discuss. However, we must go into it. You were there when it happened. You spent hours there alone with him before your mother came home. It was just a few days ago that it was the fifteenth anniversary of your father's passing. Has the anniversary weighed heavily upon you? Sometimes anniversaries can flare up residual feelings. Was that the reason you began to think about Elly again?"

Albert turned his head back towards Dr. Collins. "Please, don't mention Elly." More writing came from the good doctor after this.

"We have to discuss all the details, Albert. I was told you were going to "be with Elly". Have you been dreaming of her again?"

Albert, stone-faced, answered, "I don't know for sure. She would come to me in my dreams, yes. I was going to meet her a few nights ago. She said she and I would come together again like before."

"I see...How did you meet her before?" Dr. Collins continued to write fervently.

"We would spend our days under the palms with the tropical breeze blowing through our hair and swim in the crystal clear waters of the bay."

"Right...but how would you get there to this paradise?"

"I would enter my closet and crawl through the small door of the crawl space...except it didn't open to the crawl space it led to a dark cave that came out onto an overgrown part of the beach." Albert knew how this sounded and watched as Dr. Collins wrote out everything he was saying. He imagined him writing in bold letters - **INSANE, CRAZY, LOONY, CUCKOO**.

Dr. Collins looked up from his clipboard. "Can you describe Elly for me, please."

Albert smiled, "Sure. She's around my height, the same age as me, she has fiery red hair, fair skin, incredible style and is the most gorgeous woman that I've ever seen."

"Would you describe her as your dream girl?" Dr. Collins interjected.

"Yes, I certainly would."

Dr. Collins laid his clipboard down on the small table between them and looked very seriously at Albert. "Mr. Oden, she certainly is a dream girl. Because she's nothing but a fantasy." The smile quickly faded from Albert's face.

He sat up and began to listen further. "Elly is a creation of your mind, Albert. She doesn't exist. She never did. Every time you thought you went to see her you were only delving deep into your mind. You never physically went anywhere."

Albert took a deep breath trying to control the anger welling up within him. "You're telling me I just curled up or something and became catatonic and stayed like that the entire time I was with her?! Did anyone ever find me in this supposed state?"

The good doctor remained silent for a moment. "There was nowhere listed that you were discovered in such a state, but of course it's only logical to believe that you were. Albert, Elly doesn't exist. The sooner you admit this the sooner you'll be on the road to becoming better."

"I don't want to discuss Elly anymore with you. You'll never understand." Doctor Collins uncrossed his legs and leaned close to Albert. "Every session we have we'll be discussing "Elly". Whether you like it or not."

The anger that had been building reached a fever pitch. "I told you to LEAVE ELLY OUT OF THIS!!" Albert quickly grabbed the clipboard and gave it a pitch across the room into the good doctor's window shattering it. Albert knew what the good doctor was saying was bullshit. He could tell him over and over but he'd never understand.

Albert ended up spending another week in the padded cell for his "little stunt" as they called it. Albert hated going back there, but he accepted it.

After his week in purgatory passed he returned to hell. Candace led him back to the same room that was going to be his before. This time however he didn't see Jeremy or Leo. Thank God for small blessings.

Candace left Albert and he decided he would return to his bench outside. Maybe he would run into Elaine again. "Good to see you out and about again, my dear boy." Albert turned around and was greeted by the good doctor. "Do try not to break any more windows. My how you've been quite troublesome." Albert turned away and began walking towards the courtyard. "Oh, hold on a second! Don't be so rude, Mr. Oden. I wanted to tell you that this evening you'll be attending your first group therapy session. I do hope it goes better than our one on one session. It will be from 8:00 until 9:00 this evening in the commons room."

"I'll be there with bells on." Albert quipped.

Dr. Collins chuckled. "That's the spirit. Well, I must be going. See you around, Albert."

Albert walked outside to his bench and was a bit shocked to see Elaine sat underneath it. He walked over to her and as soon as she saw him she began to talk a mile a minute. "Everyone was talking about how you nearly killed old man Collins in his office!" She went on to say that everyone was calling him crazy and to stay away from him. She asked him if it were true. Albert laughed a bit and assured her it was blown out of proportion. She then went on to ask who Elly was.

Albert immediately stopped laughing and asked, "How do you know Elly?"

She pointed her finger across the yard to a busted window with tape over it. "When you busted old man Collins' window that clipboard of his flew out onto the ground over there and this creepy guy found it. He read through it and began spreading around what was written on it."

Albert's face dropped. He clenched his fists. "Who is this creepy guy who found it?" Albert said, trying to contain his rage.

"Oh, he's over there playing basketball. What's his name? Um, it starts with a J. Let's see…Justin? Jacob? Jerry?"

"Jeremy?" Albert interjected.

"Yes! That's it," Elaine said. "Wait, do you know him?"

Albert looked over at Jeremy and Leo playing basketball. If looks could kill. "You could say that," Albert managed.

Elaine tried to ask Albert about Elly one more time but Albert told her he wasn't going to be discussing her. She was a private matter. Elaine finally dropped it and they went to lunch shortly after.

They ended up having grilled chicken. Albert was pleased with lunch. He tried not to let what Jeremy had done get to him. He sat next to Elaine again and she continued to talk about random nonsense that Albert didn't care to listen to.

His mind was, as usual, on Elly. He had grown increasingly concerned over the fact that he hadn't seen her in any of his dreams. Most of Albert's dreams now only consisted of darkness. Could you call those dreams though? Either way, this was rather concerning to him. He felt this place was the reason behind it all.

During the previous week, they had prescribed nightly medication to help him sleep and medication during the day to keep his mind sharp. The medication did neither of those things. He had at first decided to hide his medication in his room in a fold in his mattress but Candace had found his stash after two days. Each day after she had to personally watch him take his medication. Ever since he began taking these pills daily he felt an integral part of himself begin to dull. It was stated that his mind would be sharp but he felt it was dulled. It was really beginning to depress him.

"Well, I've gotta go see my folks again," Elaine said as she placed her lunch tray on a pile with the others. Albert placed his on top of hers. "Maybe we can meet up after? There's supposed to be a movie playing in the recreation room later. Maybe we can watch it together?"

Albert smiled lightly, "Maybe." She skipped off down the hall looking pleased by Albert's response. He hoped she wasn't developing any kind of feelings towards him. She'd only get burned if she did. His heart beat for another...and she was waiting for him.

Albert returned outside to his bench of solitude. Without Elaine there running her mouth off it was pleasantly serene. The temperature was a bit warmer out today. Albert could feel spring wasn't too far off. Albert thought back to what Dr. Collins had said about group therapy that evening. He hoped that maybe he wouldn't have to talk too much. Since rumors were spread about him God only knew what people would be thinking about him.

True to her word Elaine returned outside about an hour later. She walked up to Albert with a smile on her face. "Hey, it's almost time for that movie? I found out it's gonna be The Karate Kid Part II. You still wanna go?"

Albert didn't have much interest. He hadn't seen the first Karate Kid let alone the second one. "Um, I think I'll hang back here a while," Albert said.

Elaine's smile quickly faded and she looked heartbroken over his response. "Oh, OK. I guess I'll go alone then." He could see tears forming in the corners of her eyes. She began to slowly turn and walk away.

"Wait...fine I'll go," Albert muttered.

She turned around and her smile had returned to her face. "Yeah? That's great. I was looking forward to it."

"...Yeah, I could tell." Albert stood up and put his hands into his pockets. As they walked along to the entrance back inside Elaine put her arm around his. Albert rolled his eyes a bit but went along with it for her sake.

Once they got back inside Elaine took point and led the way to the theatre room as she called it. Albert imagined a theatre of some sort with a stage and a large screen that came down with rows of red velvet seats. He found himself imagining he and Elly watching a movie sitting together with his arm around her and her smiling happily.

"We're here!" Elaine said, cutting through Albert's fantasy. She pushed the double doors open and the room couldn't possibly be any further from what he had imagined. It was a small cramped room with a dozen or so multicolored plastic chairs and a wheel in television set with a VCR underneath it. This looked like some sort of elementary school reject theatre. They did have a table with a row of snacks on it though. Albert thought that was a plus at least.

The two of them poured themselves some fruit punch and got a plate of chips and candy along with a bowl of popcorn and took their seats. A handful of other people walked in a few minutes later and did the same. Albert was a bit worried he would be sitting next to someone he didn't know or God forbid have Jeremy come strolling in but luckily he or Leo didn't show up.

The movie began and Elaine began commenting on nearly everything that was going on. Albert couldn't get into the movie even if he had wanted to. He found himself trying to drift back into that theatre with Elly and for a while, he sat there with his eyes closed trying to focus on that thought.

He found it a bit more difficult from when he had done it before though. Before he had arrived at Duke's End he could spend hours daydreaming but here it wasn't quite the same. The daydreams weren't as vivid as before. He blamed those damned pills they were forcing on him for this. Surely they must be the same pills his mother had tried passing off as vitamins. Both of them left him feeling dulled but the pills they had been giving him here were worse.

"Are you awake?" Elaine's voice cut through his thoughts yet again. His eyes opened and he nodded at her. He looked down and noticed she had grabbed his right hand. He looked up at Elaine. She smiled at him and squeezed his hand softly.

Albert frowned a bit then slowly separated his hand from hers and moved it into his pocket. She looked down obviously hurt by this. "Why don't you like me, Albert?" she said, looking into his eyes.

"I'm sorry. I should have known this might happen. I'm very much spoken for," Albert said, flatly.

She looked away from him. "By Elly? I heard about her…about how she's not real."

Albert stood up angrily. "You…don't know a damn thing about Elly so don't you dare say anything else!" Albert looked up from Elaine and could see that the movie was stopped and everyone was looking at him. "I gotta go. Goodbye, Elaine."

Albert quickly walked out of the room flinging the double doors aside and looked at the clock in the hall. It was almost supper time but he wasn't in any mood for food. He found himself a nice bench to sit on a few hallways away from the theatre next to a radiator and a window.

The window didn't offer much of a view but the radiator provided him some nice warmth. It may have felt warmer out that day but as soon as the sun set the frigid cold crept back in again. "She's not real, eh? Damn you, Dr. Collins. Ridiculous." Albert decided he wasn't going to waste any more of his time on anyone in this place. They all thought he was insane. Albert thought about what Elaine had said for a while and the accusing looks in the eyes of the rest of the people watching the movie. Their eyes haunted him more than anything else.

He stood up and wiped a bead of sweat off his forehead. Looking up at the clock across from him he saw it was time for what he dreaded the most that entire day. He made his way to the commons room that Dr. Collins had mentioned to him. The commons room was located right next door to the cafeteria. Albert had noticed it after lunch. He was glad he didn't have to wander around looking for it. He decided to wait a few minutes to let everyone clear out of the cafeteria. The last thing he needed was to run into Elaine again after that debacle.

He took his time getting down there, sauntering down the hallways as if he didn't have a worry in the world. He finally reached the door to the commons room and could see through the small window a small group gathered inside. He took a deep breath and opened the door slowly and slipped inside.

Once inside Albert could see that five guys sat around the circle in the same multicolored plastic chairs from the theatre room. One of them was dressed in a gray suit and had matching tufts of gray hair above his ears. A clipboard rested on his lap. "Come in. Come in. Have a seat. We've been expecting you, Mr. Oden. Say hello, everyone."

Albert kept his gaze facing downward until he took his seat. "Hello," everyone said in a monotone.

"Hello, Mr. Oden!" One voice spoke up, sat across from Albert in the small circle. He immediately looked up but knew who it was before he even looked. Jeremy sat directly across from him with that same smug look on his face. That's just great. This day just keeps getting better and better, Albert thought to himself as he clenched his fists inside his pockets.

"OK, guys let's get started here. Since it's your first time with us. Why don't you stand and introduce yourself, Mr. Oden!" The therapist enthusiastically spoke.

Albert could feel his cheeks get warm. He hated standing in front of groups no matter the size. He stood up and without locking his eyes on anyone said, "Hello, I'm Albert Oden." He then quickly took his seat again.

"Nice to meet you, Albert. I'm Dr. Bloom." Albert nodded his head and leaned back as everyone else introduced themselves. He found himself tuning everyone out. This formality felt like a waste of time. He had no desire to remember these guys' names...especially Jeremy's.

Once everyone finished up Dr. Bloom spoke once more, "OK, gentlemen, we're here this evening to work on your public speaking skills. So, let's talk about whatever is on your mind." Albert was transported back to school all over again. He wondered who would be called out first and prayed it wouldn't be him. All he wanted to do was go to his room and be left alone. This day was nothing but a pain in the ass. "How about you go first, Albert? Since you're our newest addition I'd like to hear about how you've found Duke's End. How have you been adjusting to being here?"

Albert took a deep breath with his gaze fixated on the chairs in front of him. "It's been…alright." Albert managed to say.

"Oh, come on, Al. You must have more to add than that," Jeremy said. He didn't see it, but Albert could sense he was still smiling. He looked up slowly and fixated his eyes upon Jeremy. Sure enough, he was sitting there with that smug grin on his face.

"Don't interrupt, Jeremy, let Albert talk."

Albert turned towards Dr. Bloom, "I've finished actually."

Dr. Bloom looked at Albert over his glasses. "Surely you have more to add than that? What's been on your mind?"

Albert wanted to say Elly, but decided upon, "I've been thinking about wanting to go home. I have business to attend to back there."

Dr. Bloom adjusted his glasses and added, "What sort of business? What line of work are you in?"

"Personal business..." Albert replied.

"Would you care to elaborate on that?"

Albert shook his head, "No. Not particularly."

Jeremy cleared his throat and began to stir in his seat. "Do you have something to add, Jeremy?"

Jeremy's grin widened revealing a set of crooked off white teeth. "Why, yes, Dr. Bloom, as a matter of fact, I do. I have it on good authority that Mr. Oden's "personal business" as he put it consists of meeting up with a red-haired woman in his dreams." Albert's head shot up and he looked at Jeremy sitting there with his arms crossed grinning from ear to ear. "What was her name again? Oh, yeah! Elly! That's it! Apparently he's gonna go curl up in his closet or some shit and imagine he's on this tropical beach somewhere!"

Albert threw his finger out towards Jeremy and pointed at him. "Don't you dare speak Elly's name, you bastard!"

Dr. Bloom tried to interject. "OK, gentlemen. Let's watch our language and take it down a notch." He came between Albert and Jeremy and tried to defuse the situation, but Jeremy continued to speak.

"What are you gonna do, big man? You know I think Elly came to me in my dreams last night. Yeah, she and I were on that beach together gettin' down. As a matter of fact, she was screamin' my name. Jeremy. Jeremy! Jeremy!!" Each time Jeremy yelled his name Albert felt a fire within him spread until it was all-consuming.

Albert lost himself and shoved Dr. Bloom aside, sending him sprawling onto several of the other guys in the circle, and darted towards Jeremy. His eyes grew wide as he quickly stood up but was knocked down again by Albert. Albert got on top of Jeremy and began to pound both fists into that smug grin of his. Throughout Albert screamed incoherently. All he could see was red. The rest of the guys in the group looked on with horror as they saw one of Jeremy's front teeth go flying across the floor.

A moment later Albert felt himself being lifted upwards. He thought maybe some of the guys were trying to drag him off of Jeremy. He turned around and thrust his fist towards the face of the one latched onto him. It connected but to Albert's surprise, it wasn't one of the guys. He had just knocked Frank's black horn-rimmed glasses off of his meaty head. At that moment he regained his senses and turned around to look at Jeremy. What he saw shocked him. He lay sprawled out upon the black carpet, his face a bloody mess. One of his front teeth was missing. Albert couldn't help but smile at this sight.

"Get him outta here damn it!" Dr. Bloom yelled from the door.

"Yes, sir. Come along now, Mr. Oden," Frank growled at him. Albert turned around one last time before he was dragged out by the arm.

"You play, you pay, you bastard," Albert whispered as he took one final look at Jeremy.

Frank dragged Albert off to the padded room. Albert knew where they were headed before they got there. He had become quite familiar with the room's padded walls and the depressing view from its window. Frank tossed him onto the floor with a grunt and slammed the door behind him. Albert sat on the edge of the bed sensing that this wasn't going to be the end of it.

A few minutes later he could hear the sound of shoes quickly moving down the hallway towards his room followed by the sound of latches opening. "My, my, my, Mr. Oden. It seems you cannot keep yourself out of trouble." Dr. Collins looked at Albert exasperated. "Jeremy is in the medical ward right now unconscious. He's missing several teeth." Albert was surprised. He thought he'd only knocked out one of them. He must have swallowed a few as well. "I don't know what to do with you, Albert."

Albert looked up at the good doctor. "How about you let me go home?"

Dr. Collins smiled, "Yes, you'd like that. Wouldn't you? Unfortunately, I can't let you leave just yet. Especially after tonight's little stunt."

"Oh, he had it coming. The guy was an ass!"

"That very well may be but that's not all you're in trouble for this evening. I also know about your scene in the theatre room! Did you know that Elaine tried to kill herself? Did you ever stop to ask why she was here? She was admitted for severe depression! Surely she must have mentioned that to you?! Albert, you have been quite busy today!"

Albert hung his head. "I had no idea why she was here. She liked to talk, but I tuned her out most of the time…"

"Albert, you'll have to excuse me for saying this, but you've become a real self-centered egotistical bastard. I have no choice but to keep you here until further notice." With that bombshell the good doctor made his exit and Albert sat there dumbfounded by what had happened that night. He thought about yelling out to Doctor Collins as he walked off down the hall, but instead fell over onto his bed and passed out.

Albert spent the next two weeks locked away in the padded room alone with his thoughts. Albert had few opportunities to leave his room during this time. He was allowed to use the restroom and go for a walk around the halls.

He was approached by Candace a few times saying that his mother had come to visit him, but each time Albert turned the opportunity down. He said he wasn't interested in seeing her and continued to stay in his room. He imagined that she would have been upset by his decision but he had no desire to see the one that had put him here not once but twice.

Over these two weeks, Albert began to notice the medication they had been throwing at him had become stronger. It was as if they wanted to keep him doped up and under their thumb.

Something else that greatly disturbed him was the fact that he still hadn't seen Elly in his dreams. Not since that disturbing dream with the darkness surrounding him and seeing her through that "window" had he seen her after. He prayed each night that when he closed his eyes that she would greet him and he could explain to her why he had never shown up that night. He imagined that she was still there under the three palms waiting for him even now.

When the day finally arrived where Albert was released from his solitary padded cell he felt zombified. Much like before Candace came into his room and informed him of the good doctor's decision to let him return to the general populace. At this point, Albert didn't care honestly. In here or out there, it was all the same to him.

When Albert returned he found himself housed in a different wing but he could feel the eyes of everyone boring into him. It seemed word had spread throughout the entire facility about him. People cleared a path and stayed far away from Albert. He didn't mind this. He enjoyed the increased isolation.

A few days later Dr. Collins paid him a visit to his room and informed him that he would be given one-on-one therapy from then on. Albert shrugged at the news and went about his day.

For the next month, Albert found himself in a stupor. Each day blended seamlessly into the next. The only thing that broke up the monotony was the therapy sessions. These sessions became the only time Albert ever spoke.

Each session played out as Albert imagined it would. He spoke and was told time and again that what he had said occurred between him and Elly were mere delusions. Albert would have fought against what was being said but he found himself devoid of the energy it would have taken to fight. He gave up on trying to get the good doctor to understand.

After weeks of being subjected to the sessions, Albert began to question whether or not what he had been saying actually happened as well. Since he had stopped seeing Elly nothing made sense anymore. He had tried to fight this but it had become increasingly difficult. The feeling that it had all been inside his head kept nagging him. He began to agree with Dr. Collins that everything was an illusion. He just didn't know what to believe anymore.

Dr. Collins became satisfied with the results from the one on one therapy. It was the middle of April now and Dr. Collins called Albert down to his office early one rainy morning. "Albert, you've shown exemplary progress. I've contacted your mother and she'll be taking you home this afternoon." Albert sat there a moment unsure of what he had just heard. "You're going home today, dear boy! What do you think of that?"

Albert looked at the good doctor and simply said, "That's great news." He forced a smile. He couldn't believe that today he'd finally be able to go home. It had been a little over two months since he had arrived. It had felt like ages had passed since then.

He returned to his room and stood in front of his window staring out upon the courtyard. The rain was falling in steady sheets outside. Within the window, he could see his reflection staring back at him. *What a lovely day to be going home. Elly...I don't know if you're still waiting for me...or if you ever were.* He turned away from the window. *No. I know that's not true. It can't be true...I'll be coming home tonight, Elly. The three palms...I gotta meet you there. I've been...waiting for you too.*

# PART III
# Under Three Palms

# Chapter 5
# Homecoming

That afternoon Albert was led to the room where everyone's possessions were held. It felt as if he were being released from prison. They returned his clothes, his watch, and wallet to him. He went into the adjoining room and slid out of the teal robe sweats and into his clothes. He came out feeling better than he had in months. It was a short-lived feeling. When he exited into the entrance hall he was immediately greeted by his mother. She ran up to Albert and wrapped her arms around him tightly. "Alby, I've missed you so much. I tried to see you so many times but you never came."

Albert sighed. "Yeah...let's just go home, Ma. I'm very tired."

"Did you miss me?" She looked up at him. Her eyes were bloodshot and full of tears.

Albert, almost a foot taller than her, looked down at her glumly. "Yeah...now let's go."

"OK, Alby." She let him go and walked towards the double doors and opened them. Albert moved swiftly. He looked around making sure Mort wasn't anywhere close by waiting to drag him back to the padded room due to some sort of mistake. Thankfully Mort was nowhere in sight.

Albert threw the doors open and breathed deep. He was finally going home. *I'm coming Elly*, he thought as he walked down the steps. He stood there a moment as the rain fell upon him. He didn't care that his jacket was getting soaked. The rain felt amazing upon his face. "You coming, Alby?" He opened his eyes and hopped into the back seat of his mother's Buick Skylark.

Albert's mother took her time driving home through the winding roads. The rain was coming down heavily now. Albert turned his head and noticed that little island with the tree on it. It's branches swung back and forth in the wind and rain. Albert hoped he would never see that tree again. His mother tried to talk to him throughout their ride home, but he didn't have much to say. "Did you make any friends?"

Albert thought to himself, *Nope, but I made a few enemies. That's for damn sure.* "No," he replied flatly.

After a few minutes she tried to string up a conversation again, "Sydney has been calling asking how you've been doing. You should give him a call tomorrow."

"Yeah...maybe I will."

"You're like a brother to him you know. He's missed you." Albert looked out the window once more. The woods were beginning to thin out. They'd be home soon...thankfully. Albert sat there patiently listening to the sound of the rain on the car and the steady motion of the windshield wipers.

His mother pulled into their driveway ten minutes later and Albert stepped out onto the concrete feeling like he'd been away for years. He couldn't quite understand why but being back here just felt different. Something in the air had changed. He tried to shrug it off as he walked along the path to the door but couldn't. He looked up into the darkening sky as the final rays of sunlight were masked behind the thick storm clouds above. One of the clouds produced a jagged bolt of lightning.

His mother opened the front door and he stepped inside slipping out of his wet sneakers. The house felt damp and cool. All of the lights were off and it was almost pitch black inside. He walked down the darkened hallway to his domain. The place he'd been wanting to return to for months. He went to grab his door handle but found it strange when he found his door was already open. He imagined his mother must have come in to clean or change his bedsheets. He moved his hand left to the light switch and the light flicked on overhead.

A moment later when Albert's eyes adjusted to the bright light he could see that his door wasn't just open but that it had been removed. What was even more upsetting was the fact that his television set that had been sitting upon his desk was missing as well. "MA!" Albert yelled out angrily. He turned around to call out to her again but she was already standing in his doorway. She stood there in silence. Her eyes looked downward at the floor. "What…happened here? Where's my TV?!"

She took a deep breath and put her hands on her hips, "Your door is missing and the TV is the first thing you ask about? Alby…I was worried about you. I…found out it wasn't working so I took it to the curb."

Albert turned around trying to mask his rage. His body trembled as he tried to contain his anger. "Why would you do this? There was nothing wrong with that TV."

"Albert, I tried repeatedly to turn it on and it would never do anything. So, I decided to get rid of the thing. Either way, Alby, you didn't need it. You're better off without it."

"Ma…just go. I wanna be alone. I need some time to…readjust."

She turned and before she left replied, "It's good to have you home. I love you, Alby." His mother slowly walked up the hallway and Albert stood there for a moment. He shut his eyes and began to feel the anger within himself subside and he felt sadness slowly beginning to take its place. Albert sat at the foot of his bed staring at the place where his television had once sat and began to cry. *Now, what the hell am I supposed to do?!* he thought as he tried not to draw attention to himself.

He got up and turned the light off and crawled into bed. The sound of the rain outside of his window helped lull him to sleep. That night there was no Elly yet again…only the darkness that stretched out infinitely before him.

Albert was woken the next day to his mother shaking his shoulder. "You have a phone call, Alby."

Not even half awake Albert grunted something along the lines of, "Alright." to her and took the handset from her. He mumbled a "Hello?" into the receiver and was greeted by a jovial voice on the other end of the line.

"Good morning, dear boy! How are you holding up?" Albert's eyes flew open. For one brief moment, he had thought he was back at Duke's End. He thought somehow they had come for him in the night and he was right back there in that padded room once more. To his relief, he looked around and noticed he was home in his bed. He was in his room far away from that godforsaken place. Not far enough though to Albert's liking. "Are you there, Albert?"

Albert cleared his throat, "Yes, I'm here. What…do you want?"

"Nice to hear from you too, Albert," The good doctor said, clearly hurt by Albert's rudeness. Albert didn't reply further. The good doctor continued, "Well, I'm calling because I wanted to let you know we've set you up with a job. I spoke with your mother about it and she agreed it'd be a wonderful idea for you to get out of the house more and socialize and earn a bit of money for yourself. Albert immediately felt great apprehension about the prospect. He was happy to just stay home and try to figure his life out. Now he had to go out and hold down a job on top of all that?

"Where? Where am I going to be working?" Albert managed a few moments later.

"Oh, yes! I failed to mention WHERE you would be working! I do apologize. The Lando Community Library! Yes, I feel it will be a great fit for you." Albert felt even more apprehension at this. Albert was content to stay away from the LCL indefinitely after what had happened the last time he set foot in there. It had only been a few months. Surely people would still remember...and what about Yvonne? Would he be working with her? His mind became a whirlwind of thoughts. "Albert? Are you still there, my dear boy? Hello?"

Albert was brought out of his inner whirlwind by the good doctor's voice. "Yes, I'm here..."

"OK, I thought I lost you. You start tomorrow at 9 AM and work until 5. Since tomorrow is Friday I thought you could get your feet wet with just one day this week and start your full schedule next week. I do hope you have a great first day tomorrow. Get some sleep and try not to worry. You'll do just fine, dear boy. I must be going, but if you need me I'm only a phone call away. Take care, Albert." With that, the good doctor hung up and Albert sat in silence. He didn't protest the idea. He felt it would be an exercise in futility. He had learned not to protest anything the good doctor had to say because it went in one ear and out the other.

KNOCK KNOCK "Can I come in?" his mother said from out in the hall.

"You may as well. What's stopping you? Not like I have a door," Albert said, falling back into bed and turning over on his side facing the wall.

His mother came in slowly. "Don't be grouchy, Alby. What do you think of the news, Dr. Collins had to say?" I'm over the moon about it, Albert thought grimacing with his eyes closed tightly. "Are you happy about it? I thought you might be because I know how much you love the library."

"I'm not being grouchy. It's one thing to love somewhere and something entirely different to work there."

"Well, I think it'll be good for you."

"Oh, yeah? Just like Duke's End was good for me? Please...just go."

Albert could hear his mother begin to sniffle. He could tell she was crying. "Alright, I'll go. I want you to know that I took some time off of work to spend with you for a few weeks. I'm planning on cooking your favorite tonight for supper...I love you."

She turned and walked out. Albert listened to her footsteps fade as she walked down the hall. Albert lay there for a while feeling a mixture of justified anger towards his mother and shame at what he had said to her. These thoughts kept the apprehension at bay for a while at what lay ahead of him the following day. It wasn't long before the thoughts came flooding back though and Albert found the prospect of his favorite supper the furthest thing from his mind.

That night he sat across from his mother. She stared at him with a bright smile on her face. It was a face he had once felt great joy in seeing each day. He felt nothing but contempt for her now. She kept asking after every few bites if he enjoyed his meal. It took all of Albert's will to not yell at her to stop asking if he liked it. She knew it was his favorite meal. She didn't need to ask if he enjoyed it. Maybe she thought his time in Duke's End had scrambled his brains and turned him into a different person? Hell, maybe it had? Albert couldn't deny he certainly didn't feel the same as he had before. He felt so much anger deep within himself. *If only Elly were here...* Albert pushed the thought of her from his mind. *Elly...doesn't exist...right?*

Albert, moved the half-eaten steak and baked potato away from him and excused himself from the table. His mother called out to him but he simply couldn't deal with her on top of the conflict taking place within himself. Albert tossed the blankets aside and fell onto the soft mattress. He prayed sleep would come for him. He didn't even mind the darkness as long as he could simply not exist for a while.

The next morning Albert awoke to the smell of fried bacon and eggs. "Alby?" his mother said from his doorway, "Are you awake?"

Albert shuffled a bit underneath his sheets and grumbled a simple, "Yeah." in response.

"Breakfast is ready. Come and get some. It's 8 AM and you've got an hour until your first day begins." His mother walked away then. Her footsteps produced creaks from the boards beneath the beige carpeting which ran from outside his bedroom throughout their living room.

Albert lay there in his bed hidden under his sheets. He felt overwhelmed by the thought of having to go back to the library. *Damn them all. I don't need to do this…why can't they just leave me the hell alone?* Albert thought as he heard his mother's footsteps coming back down the hallway. "Alby, up, up, up! You've gotta get ready."

"Fine! I'm getting up," Albert said, throwing the sheets off of himself and motioning for his mother to leave. She nodded at him and left him to prepare. He opened his closet and pulled a random cardigan out and a t-shirt along with a pair of jeans. *Good enough*, he thought as he hastily threw on his outfit for the day. He stepped across the hall into the bathroom and flicked the light on and looked at himself in the mirror. He noticed the stubble coming in on his face. *Whatever. What does it matter really…* he shrugged as he shut the light off.

He sat down to the dining room table where his breakfast already waited for him. Beside the plate was a white pill, his vitamin for the day his mother had affectionately called it all those years. He didn't want to take the damn thing, but his mother sat across from him. She stared at him as he ate his breakfast. Albert ate all of his bacon and eggs and saved the pill for last. "Don't forget your vitamin, Alby," she said, smiling.

"I know it's not a vitamin, Ma. Why not just call it what it is? They're my crazy pills." He grabbed the pill and threw it into his mouth following it with a bit of orange juice. Albert didn't swallow the pill though. He tucked it beneath his tongue.

She arose from the table pretending not to hear what he had said. "Let's go, Alby. You want to be there early for your first day."

"Hold on. I'm gonna use the restroom." Albert walked into the dark bathroom and spit the pill into the toilet following it with a quick flush. *If I'm gonna do this. I'm not going to feel like a damn zombie.* He stepped back out into the hallway finding his mother waiting by the door.

Albert stepped outside into the cool, damp early morning air. The crisp light from the sun shone down through slants within the tree branches across the road. He spotted an older couple out for an early morning jog wearing matching gray sweatsuits.

He hopped into the back seat and tried not to think about the day ahead of him. He just wanted to take things one step at a time. It was a quick ride down to the LCL from Albert's home. As they drove through the city streets Albert noticed the countless flowers in full bloom. *New life...I wish I could have a new life.* His thoughts were quickly interrupted by the sight of the large Lando Community Library building. The building took up an entire city block in uptown Lando. Albert's mother pulled around to the side of the large building to the adjoining parking lot. "Want me to walk you in?"

"No." Albert hopped out of the car and ran for the sidewalk leading to the front entrance.

"Alby! Wait!" He turned around to see his mother had a brown paper bag in her hand. He walked back to the car and grabbed it from her. "You were about to forget your lunch! It's leftovers from last night."

"Thanks." She gave him a quick hug and tried to kiss the top of his head but he broke free and took off for the sidewalk once again.

Stepping into the vestibule, Albert's footsteps echoed loudly announcing his presence long before he made it to the front desk. "Good morning, Albert! It's been a long time! We're so happy to see you back and to have you working with us now!" Delores' chipper voice made Albert feel slightly more at ease. He had always liked Delores. She was always so bright and content with being there at the library ever since he was a small boy.

"Good morning," Albert replied. He was waiting for her to possibly say something about the spectacle he had made of himself last time.

"Come on around behind the counter. I'll give you a little tour." Albert walked around behind the counter as he was asked. During the quick tour, Delores showed Albert around "behind the scenes" as she called it. He got to take a look at things he'd grown so accustomed to seeing from a different angle. One of the things he found the most interesting was something simple, yet so mysterious. He got to see the book return slot in action.

"Hi, Albert, how have you been doing?"

Albert turned and greeted Sheila. "Hi, there. I've been alright. It's my first day…"

"Oh, yes. I know! We're so glad to have you here. We've been needing someone for a long while. A girl we hired back in the fall left us after New Years to go back to school and that left us kind of short-handed for a while. Yvonne, her name was. Maybe you saw her here a few times?" *Oh…I SAW her alright*, Albert thought to himself, feeling immediate relief at the news that he wouldn't be running into her here. "Anyway, we're glad to have you here." Sheila smiled brightly. "I'll be taking over from Delores now. I'll explain to you the responsibilities you'll have while working here. One of which is right here." She walked over to the book return cart positioned underneath the slot. "It's your main responsibility to take this cart and organize the books within it and return them to their proper places within the stacks out on the floor. Follow me."

Sheila grabbed the cart and began to wheel it through the back offices to the front counter. She took one of the books out and walked Albert through the process of locating its proper location within the stacks. Albert watched and made mental notes of everything. It was all pretty simple though. "OK, Albert, I think that does it. Oh, one more thing I wanted to mention. I'm the new director of the library. Dr. Shields retired at the end of last year." Albert could vaguely remember Dr. Shields. She always seemed rather unfriendly towards him so he never really cared for her.

"Congratulations," he replied.

"Thanks, Albert. I just wanted to share that with you so you know if you have any questions regarding your pay or other work-related questions you can come to me. Alright, have fun. If you need anything Delores or me won't be too far." Albert nodded his head and Sheila returned to the back offices.

Albert stood there for a moment eyeballing the large stack of books in front of him. "Let's get started," he said to himself, wheeling the cart out of the open. Delores waved to him as he pushed the cart towards the back and out of sight. He waved back right before he turned the corner.

Once he had turned the corner he found himself in a place he remembered all too well. He stopped the cart and pushed it against one of the shelves. It was the same shelf Yvonne had stocked that day...he could see a large stain upon the carpet from his chicken soup. *What a day that was. What the hell was I thinking? I was such a fool. I'm so sorry, Elly.*

He stood there staring at the stain for a moment longer until he heard the sound of footsteps. An older man came around the corner looking at the books. He looked at Albert and gave him a quick nod and a smile. Albert returned the gesture then grabbed his cart and moved around the corner. He was happy the man came along. It wasn't good for him to be thinking back on that day. Lord knows he spent enough time after Christmas doing that.

Albert tried to keep his mind preoccupied the rest of the day and stay away from that part of the library as best he could. He took note of a few interesting books he thought he could check out over the weekend at the end of his shift.

As he slowly went through his work his stomach began to growl. He pushed his cart into a corner behind the reference books and approached Delores. "Hi, Albert. How's it coming out there? Do you have a question?"

"It's coming along alright. I did have a quick question though. When can I take my lunch?"

"Oh, bless your heart. You can take it now, dear. Go ahead." Albert thanked her and decided to take his lunch out to the small reading garden in the back of the library. The garden had always intrigued him but he'd never stepped foot out there before.

With his lunch in tow, he exited out into the pleasantly warm afternoon air. He sat down on a wooden bench shielded from the noonday sun and opened his bag. He quickly ate the remains of his steak and baked potato from the previous night and then stood up and stretched. He sat back down and closed his eyes and listened to the sounds of birds chirping away in the tree limbs overhead and within the distance.

As Albert sat there he began to feel the warmth of the sun shining through the newly sprouted leaves above him. He felt himself drifting further and further away.

*"Come on, Alligator! I wanna show you something!" Al could feel the beige carpet beneath his small toes and jumped into his father's arms upon the couch. "Whoa, slow it down there."*

*"What are we gonna look at, Daddy?"*

*Al's father grabbed the remote sitting upon the coffee table. "I'm going to show you paradise, Al."*

*Al's eyes grew wide with wonder. "What's that?" Al asked.*

*"Ho, ho! You'll see, my son." His father pressed a button and the screen flashed on. Upon the screen, little Al watched as a beach came into view from a balcony window. He could hear the laughter of his mother and father in the background.*

*The scene jumped then to a shot of the sun hanging low in the sky above a bay of shimmering crystal clear water. The camera panned out revealing platinum white sands and a woman sat upon a wooden beach chair. The camera drew closer to her as she turned around smiling ear to ear. It was his mother. She looked so young and beautiful sitting there. Her normally long hair was cut short with long bangs. Little Al sat there watching as the sun slowly set upon a world he discovered that day...paradise.*

*He turned back to look at his father but his father wasn't sitting behind him any longer. He was lying face-first on the beige carpet. He ran to him and began to shake him. A hand fell softly upon his shoulder. He turned to see who it was. Elly stood above him. She looked down upon young Al with a warm smile upon her face and spoke, "Wake up, love."*

"Yo, Albert. Wake up!" Albert fell off the bench onto the cobblestone below.

"Ow," he could only manage.

"Damn, you OK, Al?" It was Sydney, but what was he doing there?

"Syd? What the...what's going on?" Albert turned over and looked up at Sydney. His arm was extended offering to help him up. Albert grabbed his hand and rose back to his feet then sat back down upon the bench.

"You looked like you were having a bad dream. You were twitching and moaning and everything."

*How long have I been out here?* He looked at his watch. '12:50'. He had been sitting there a good forty-five minutes. Albert could hardly remember what had just happened to him. Bits and pieces were there but he couldn't put them together. "Yeah, I'm alright. What are you doing here?"

Sydney took a seat next to Albert. "I called your house wanting to check up on you and your mom said you were down here working! Hey, man, you got a job! That's great. So, I decided to drop in on you. The lady at the counter said she saw you go out here when I asked where you were so here I am."

Albert nodded. "Ah, I see..." Albert could tell that Sydney seemed like he had something else on his mind. "Is there anything else? You seem like you have something on your mind."

Sydney laughed to himself. "You know me so well. Yeah, I do. Look I know you were away for a long while and I wanted to treat you to a night on the town tonight. A guys night out if you will. What do you say?"

"By night out on the town I assume you mean going down to The Sexothèque?"

Sydney scratched the back of his head. "Um...well, come to think of it, they do have a special tonight...bring a friend and get half off."

Albert sat there a moment gazing up into the trees. "Sure...I'll go."

Sydney arose from the bench shaking his head. "Ah, I figured you'd say that, but I...Wait...YOU'LL GO?!" Albert nodded yes. "Hot damn! I never thought I'd see the day!" *Me neither*, Albert thought. "You're not gonna regret this! You get off at five. Your mom told me. I'll be out in the parking lot waiting for you. I'll let your mom know don't worry. I'll let you get back to work for now. Ah, this is gonna be great!" Sydney almost skipped out of the reading garden back into the library.

*Waiting for me, huh? Have I made a mistake? I just don't know...but going home tonight just doesn't feel like where I need to be...* Albert had many thoughts which he mused about during the rest of his shift. His decision had been made. Like it or not...Albert was going to The Sexothèque.

# Chapter 6
# The Sexothèque

Albert clocked out at five and took his time walking towards the front door. He entered the late afternoon air and stood a moment looking left to right. He weighed his options. Should I just walk home? I'm sure Syd wouldn't mind if I stood him up. "To hell with this," Albert muttered to himself and began walking towards the crosswalk.

"Yo, Al, where you headed?!" Albert stopped in his tracks and slowly turned around. Sydney was leaning against the light brown brick of the front of the building with a perplexed look on his face. Albert waved and begrudgingly walked towards him. "Were you taking the scenic route, Al? Either way, we gotta go! They'll be opening in about twenty minutes." Sydney was decked out in a flashy red dress shirt with a black tie and black dress pants. Albert felt a bit underdressed but followed Sydney around the corner to his car.

Sydney owned a small red Mazda Miata which he loved leaving the top down on even during the winter. Today was no exception. Once Sydney reached his door he hopped into the driver's seat and started it up. Albert slowly took his seat and closed the door behind him. "You ready for the night of your life, Al?!" Sydney yelled.

"Ummm..." Albert said, already feeling he'd made a grave mistake.

"I'll take that as hell yeah!" Sydney shifted and hit the gas. *Dear God. What have I gotten myself into!* Albert thought as Sydney sped out onto the road cutting off a blue minivan. The driver of the minivan honked the horn and Sydney quickly threw up his right hand above him promptly flipping it off. Sydney continued to speed down Broadway towards downtown laughing maniacally.

Broadway was a long stretch of road that had many privately run local businesses. They were the lifeblood of the local economy. You could find anything along this stretch of road from Aaron Bail Bonds to Zed's Bike Shop but as Sydney flew down the stretch it was all a blur to Albert. He closed his eyes and just held on for the ride.

The car came to a stop and Sydney killed the engine. "We're here, buddy." Albert opened his eyes to see a large building with bright neon signs on the front reading, 'Sexothèque'. *So this is it,* Albert thought as he exited the Miata. Sydney came around and slapped Albert on the back. "You ready? Let's head on inside, Al."

In truth, Albert was far from ready but he took a deep breath and followed as Sydney walked up the sidewalk to the front door. As they drew closer to the door Albert could hear the muffled sound of what sounded like disco music. Sydney threw the doors open and stepped inside. "Good evening, ladies!" he yelled out. Albert took one last breath and pushed one of the doors aside and entered.

Albert looked over the place. It was decked out in gold and neon galore. Above the stage hung a giant disco ball casting hundreds of fragments of light in all directions. The whole place was a relic from a bygone era. Upon the stage Albert noticed a woman stark naked clinging to a pole and he quickly averted his eyes. What did he expect really, but he still wasn't quite prepared for what he had seen. "What do you think, Al?!" Sydney yelled over the thumping bass filled disco tune that was playing. "You want me to set you up with one of the girls?! They all know me! Just pick one out!"

Albert's face began to turn red. "Ummm, I think I'll just have a drink to start!" Albert yelled as the music faded.

"Alright, bro. The bar's over there. Tell Joe you're with me. He'll set you right up."

Albert wasn't much of a drinker. He tended to only drink if Sydney offered him something which is what he had done the year prior on Albert's birthday. Albert had turned 21 and Sydney brought him a bottle of saké he had ordered from Japan to celebrate. Albert reluctantly drank it but in the end, Sydney drank the most of it. That had been the last time Albert had had a drink.

He took a seat upon one of the worn red leather bar stools and looked at the large mirror behind the bar. He could see Syd wasn't wasting any time and was already tossing some bills at the woman on stage. He couldn't help but laugh a bit at the spectacle he was making of himself.

"Good evening, sir. What'll it be?" Albert looked at the barkeep, a middle-aged man with a well-worn face almost matching the barstool he was currently sat upon. This thought also made Albert chuckle a bit. The barkeep smiled in return. "First timer? I saw you stumble in with Syd there. He's one of our best customers. Good guy…great tipper."

"He's my cousin." Albert had to almost yell as the next disco tune cut in with loud bell chimes.

"Is that right? Well, what's your name, sir?"
"Albert!"

"Nice to meet you, Al. I'm Joe." Joe presented his hand and Albert firmly grasped it and shook it looking Joe in the eye. "That's a man's handshake right there. So, you thought about that drink yet, Al?" One drink sprang to his mind. One he had been curious about for quite some time.

"I'll take a mojito."

"One mojito coming up." Albert watched as Joe made his mojito and set it down in front of him upon the bar. "Enjoy your drink, Al." Albert stared at the drink for a moment before taking a small sip. The mint immediately hit his taste buds. Albert took another larger sip and looked up to see what Sydney was up too. He could see him talking with the girl who was dancing on stage at a table across the club. He stared down into his drink. It was pretty tasty…but he imagined Elly's would have been better. He let out an audible sigh.

"What's wrong, sugar?" a woman said behind Albert. "You're over here all by your lonesome." She quickly took a seat upon the stool next to Albert's. He turned to look at her and much as the woman on stage had been she too was completely nude. Albert's eyes grew wide and he turned but not without giving her a quick involuntary once over. Her ebony skin glistened in the light of the rotating disco ball. "Don't feel bad about lookin', sugar. It's alright."

"I'm sorry. I'm just not used to a place like this."

"Oh, this is your first time? I thought so. I knew I hadn't seen ya before!"

"Yeah, I was invited by my cousin Sydney," Albert muttered.

"Sydney's your cousin? Oh, wow. Every one of the girls knows Syd!"

Albert shook his head. "That's what he said."

"Yeah, he's a real character. So, what are you doing over here by yourself? Why don't you come on over with Syd and we can all have fun together?"

Albert thought about this a moment then Elly's face flashed in his mind. "I…can't. I'm with someone."

"Oh? Why aren't you with them tonight, sugar?"

"I wish I was…she's gone now, though, gone away…To a place where we can't meet again."

"Oh...I'm so sorry to hear that."

"And now, gentlemen, allow me to introduce the lovely Olivia!" The deejay announced loudly as the woman quickly stood up.

"Oh, crap. I'm sorry. I gotta get up there. I'll be back though soon. I'm Olivia by the way!"

"I'm Albert!"

"Pleasure meeting you, Albert!" Olivia yelled as she quickly ran for the door alongside the stage. Albert was amazed at how fast she moved in those stiletto heels.

As the night ticked by Albert sat to the bar nursing his mojito and listening to the thumping disco tunes blaring. Pretty soon Albert found himself becoming enraptured by the music. The thumping bass lines and synths pulsated in his bloodstream and he felt alive again. Olivia would come and chat with him between her sets. Albert mainly sat there as she did most of the talking. She didn't seem to mind. Albert had grown used to the role of listening. It reminded him of his time at Duke's End...He momentarily thought of Elaine and hoped wherever she was out there tonight that she was alright...Olivia moved her stool close to Albert's and periodically would touch his shoulder. He kept his gaze averted from her but sometimes his gaze would shift to her shoulder-length curly black hair. Sometimes he would catch hints of coconut wafting in the air when she would walk up. Before Albert knew it he had put away four mojitos and was feeling a bit out of it.

"Yo, Al. It's time to head out, bro," Sydney said, walking up to the bar and slapping Albert upon his back.

Albert looked at his watch, '5:45 AM'. "First to arrive, last to leave," Albert muttered as he slid off his stool and onto his feet.

"You got that right! Damn, what a night! Hey, Sharon and I were gonna go out for some breakfast at Denny's. I saw you chatting up Olivia all night. I'm proud of ya, bro! Why don't you invite her too?!" Albert frowned and was about to say no, but Sydney saw what he was about to say and took matters into his own hands. "Yo, Olivia. You wanna get a bite to eat with us?!" Sydney yelled across the club. "Sure thing, Syd. I'd love to! Just let me change real quick." Sydney looked at Albert. "You'll thank me later. She's a really nice girl." Albert frowned but as he had done pretty much all night he went along for the ride.

Albert sauntered out into the early April morning air outside of The Sexothèque. The sun was just peeking out over the tops of the buildings surrounding this little nook of downtown Lando. He breathed a deep breath and staggered backward a step. *Damn, those mojitos hit me more than I thought they would.* "You alright there, Al?" Sydney said as he pushed the doors aside, walking out with his arm around a woman with short black hair wearing a skin-tight black dress that sparkled in the morning light. Albert had watched Sydney with her all night in the corner and watched as the two walked back to the VIP rooms in the back.

"Yeah, I just need a bite to eat and some sleep."

"Haha! Well, I'll get you home soon, but first things first - the food! Oh, where are my manners? Allow me to introduce the lovely Miss Sharon Moon. Sharon, this is Albert. Albert, this is Sharon."

Albert lowered his head and said, "Nice to meet you, Sharon. I'm Syd's cousin Albert."

Sharon smiled and replied, "It's very nice to meet you, Albert. Syd has mentioned you a fair amount. He's been trying to get you to join us for quite some time."

"Yes, babe, and he *FINALLY* decided to grace us with his presence tonight. Now that the introductions are out of the way, where's Olivia?" Just as Sydney uttered those words Olivia pushed the doors aside and the early morning sun hit her. She had on a pair of oversized heart sunglasses and a bright red bodycon dress. For a moment, as she stood there in the early morning rays of the sun, she appeared to be glowing. Albert couldn't help but feel a bit captivated. She turned toward him and flashed him a quick smile. He quickly turned away from her. He could feel the guilt begin to tug at his heart again.

"Alright, now that everyone is present and accounted for..." Sydney threw an annoyed look towards Olivia. "We can finally head on over to Denny's." Olivia promptly shot Sydney a bird followed by the two of them having a great laugh. Albert began to walk down the street towards Sydney's Miata when Sydney yelled out to him. "Yo, Al, I was gonna take Sharon with me over to Denny's. How about you ride with Olivia?" Albert could see that this wasn't a request as Sydney came walking up with his arm still around Sharon.

He opened the passenger door for her and closed it. "Such a gentleman," Sharon said, lightly giggling.

"Oh, yeah. You know it, babe," Sydney replied with a confident look on his face. "Al, don't keep the lady waiting. We'll see ya over there in a few."

Albert turned around and could see Olivia waiting by the curb next to a lime green hardtop Jeep. She waved to him, "Albert, come on over. I don't bite." Sydney hopped into the Miata and quickly started it up and sped off down the street. Sharon let out a playful scream as they sped away into the distance. Albert walked up the street a bit to Olivia.

"Nice Jeep," he said, quickly.

"Thanks. I've had it for a few years now." She got behind the wheel and Albert hopped into the passenger seat. She started it up and music immediately began playing. "I hope you don't mind the disco. I got D.B. to make me a mixtape a while back."

"Who's D.B.?" Albert looked over at her perplexed.

"Right. I'm sorry. He's the deejay at The Sexothèque. He was the guy on the mic all night."

"Ahh, I see. He's got some good taste in music I must say."

"You like disco too?" Olivia lit up and began to discuss her love of disco with Albert. He listened as she drove through the desolate early morning streets.

As they pulled up into the parking lot at Denny's Olivia was still raving about the various disco tracks she discovered while working at The Sexothèque. "Well, we're here! I'm sorry, Albert. When I get to talking I just can't seem to stop sometimes."

"No need to apologize. I enjoyed hearing about the songs."

Olivia smiled brightly. "That's good. Maybe I can get D.B. to make you a mixtape too?"

Albert smiled at her. "Yeah, that would be pretty cool."

Olivia reached over and lightly touched Albert's arm. "You're so easy to talk to, Albert." Albert blushed and looked away from her.

"Let's head in. I can see Sydney and Sharon by the window there," Albert said, pointing at Sydney.

"Oh, yeah! Let's head on in." The two exited Olivia's Jeep and walked alongside the sidewalk to the front door. They passed the window in which Sydney and Sharon were sat by. As they did so both Sydney and Sharon shot a quick bird at Olivia and began to smile cheekily. Olivia promptly began to laugh. She composed herself and the two entered into the chilly diner.

Olivia quickly grabbed onto Albert's arm. "Brrr! It's like an icebox in here." Albert felt her warm skin pressing onto him and could feel his cheeks begin to turn red. Olivia relinquished her grip on Albert's left arm once they reached the booth. Olivia slid into the booth across from Sharon and Albert took his seat across from Sydney.

"It's about time you guys showed up. What was the hold-up, Olivia? You and Al here get more acquainted?"

Olivia rolled her eyes. "If you must know I was talking disco with Albert."

"Ohh, lord. Now you've gone and done it, Al. You get this one started on disco and she won't shut up about it."

"Fuck you, Syd. Albert liked the conversation."

Sydney turned toward Albert with wide eyes. "That's not true! Say it isn't so, Al!"

Albert leaned back and replied, "Actually, I quite enjoyed the music tonight." He quickly began to look through the menu. Sydney began to rave about how disco was dead but Albert tuned him out.

He tuned out everyone really until the waitress came over to the table to take their orders. It was then that a familiar voice spoke and broke through to Albert. "Is everybody ready?"

"Give us a few more minutes," Olivia replied. Albert looked up from his menu and set his eyes upon someone who he hadn't expected to see. Yvonne walked back to the other side of the diner and began to chat with another familiar face. *Dear God...it's Clayton.* Clayton sat in a booth next to the entrance. Across from him on the opposite side of the table lay a pile of textbooks and various notebooks sprawled out. Yvonne slid into the booth for a moment and jotted a few things down after flipping through the largest textbook. *I gotta get the hell outta here.* Is all Albert could think at this moment.

"Syd...I don't feel so well all of a sudden. I don't think the drinks are sitting well. I wanna go home. Could you take me home, please?"

"What?! We just got here. You seemed alright a few minutes ago...although you do kinda look a bit paler than usual."

Olivia moved closer to Albert in the booth. "Are you gonna be OK, Albert?" Olivia looked at him over the tops of her sunglasses. Her dark brown eyes showed deep concern.

"Yes, I just need to lie down. I'm sorry, guys." Albert gave another quick look over to Clayton and Yvonne. *She'll be back any minute.*

"Syd, it's alright. You can go ahead and run Albert home. He is looking a bit ill," Sharon said, lightly holding onto Sydney's arm.

"Fine...I guess I'll take ya home, ya lightweight. Let's roll, Al. Sharon, I hate to cut our time short. I'll see you soon," Sydney said as he gave her a quick wink then leaned in and kissed her.

"OK, Syd, hurry on out. Albert looks like he's getting worse," Sharon said. "It was nice to finally meet you, Albert. I hope you get to feeling better."

"Thanks, Sharon. It was nice meeting you too," Albert said as he quickly rose from the booth and took one step but was stopped by one final question from Olivia.

"Hey, Albert, will you be coming back next week?"

Before Albert could think about it he quickly blurted out, "Maybe. We'll see. Bye for now." Albert made a beeline for the door. As he got closer to the door he tried to be as inconspicuous as possible.

"Yo, Al, wait up!" *Damn it, Syd! Keep it down!* Albert thought as Clayton looked over at him.

"Hey! I know you."

Albert stood frozen for a moment, his hand about to push the door open. "No, you don't," he replied, hastily throwing open the door and running towards Sydney's Miata. He hopped into the passenger seat followed by Sydney.

"Yo, you know that guy, Al? He looked kinda pissed off. Damn, he's coming out..." Albert could see Clayton coming out of Denny's with an angry look upon his face.

"I don't know him, and I don't wanna know him. Punch it, Syd!"

"You don't gotta tell me twice!" Sydney punched the gas and threw his right arm up raising his middle finger high into the air. "Man, what an asshole. Probably drunk as a skunk."

"…Yeah, for sure," Albert muttered as he looked through the rearview mirror. He could see Clayton flipping the bird in return.

As Sydney drove through the increasing traffic he drove past an apartment complex. "What the…shit!" He put the brakes on and turned into the apartment's parking lot.

"What is it, Syd?" Albert asked, looking around. "Wait…isn't this your apartment building?"

"Yeah, it is." He parked next to a bright yellow Chevrolet Cavalier. "That's Victoria's car. She's not supposed to be back until tonight! Fuck…." He killed the engine and sat there a moment then snapped his fingers. "I've got it! I can imagine she must be there in the living room wondering where I've gone too. Come upstairs with me, Al. I'll tell her I was out with you last night. She won't suspect we were up to anything untoward."

"Untoward, eh? Word of the day," Albert laughed.

"This is serious, Al. I need you to come up with me right now."

"Alright. Let's go...but I really must be getting home." Sydney hopped out of the car. "This won't take long. This ain't a social call." Albert glanced up at the apartment complex bathed in the golden morning light. Within the complex, Victoria sat in the shadows waiting. Albert thought this to himself as he began to climb the stairs.

Sydney's apartment was located on the second floor. Albert had only been over to Sydney's place one time shortly after he had moved in about a year prior. Sydney and Victoria had met in middle school but Albert only spoke to her now and then. She had always been a bit of a silly girl, cracking jokes with Sydney all the time. Albert recalled she had slightly wavy dark brown hair to her shoulders and soft brown eyes. For the life of him, he didn't understand why Sydney frequented The Sexothèque when he had Victoria at home. The two arrived outside of the apartment door and Sydney grabbed his keys from his back pocket.

He slowly opened the door and entered the darkened living room. It was just as Albert had envisioned it. Albert remained in the hallway for a moment when a lamp lit up across from Sydney. "Hi, Syd. I've been waiting up for you." Albert heard Victoria say quietly.

"OH! Hi, sweetheart! I didn't know you were coming in last night. If I'd have known I would have canceled my plans."

"I tried calling your cell throughout the night. Where were you?"

"Oh, I left my cell here by mistake...I'm sorry."

"Can you close the door, please. Why'd you leave it open behind you?"

"Because…" Sydney made a motion for Albert to come in, "…I was out with this guy last night. We were over at his place catching up." Albert slowly walked in and waved to Victoria. She was sitting on the recliner wearing a black t-shirt with neon Palm trees on it and a pair of pajama pants. Next to the recliner, Albert could see the lamp she had turned on which dimly lit the room.

She looked surprised to see Albert. "Oh, hi, Albert. It's been a while. I didn't know Syd was going over to see you."

"Neither did I until the last minute," Albert said.

"You know how I am, baby. I live in the moment sometimes. I'm so sorry that you were waiting all night for me. I'll make it up to you. How's dinner at John's sound? A nice big juicy steak?"

Victoria's dour expression instantly lifted at this. "And a nice cheesecake for dessert?" she cooed.

"Yes, of course!"

"OK, I'm looking forward to that."

"Me too, Vicky. Hey, let me run Albert home real quick. I was gonna have him crash here, but since you're here I'll take him back home so we can have some alone time," he said, winking twice at her.

"Hehe. Syd, stop it." Victoria blushed. "OK, go on. It's good seeing you again, Albert. You should come back over for supper some night soon."

"Good seeing you too, Victoria. I might just do that." Albert waved goodbye and stepped back out into the hallway.

Sydney blew a kiss. "Bye, Vicky. Love you."

Victoria replied with, "Love you too, darling." and then they were off.

Sydney pulled up into Albert's driveway and looked over at him. "Thanks again, Al. I don't know what I'd have done without you."

"Tell the truth possibly?"

Sydney let out a forced laugh. "Take care, Al. We had a hell of a time last night. Didn't we?"

"...Yeah, we did," Albert said, stepping out of the car, "Take it easy, Syd."

"Like Sunday mornin'." Sydney laughed maniacally as he backed up onto the street and sped off. Albert looked up into the cloudless, deep blue sky above for a moment then made his way back inside.

When he closed the front door the house was as quiet as the grave. He was surprised his mother wasn't sitting there as Victoria had been to Sydney but she wasn't. In all honesty, he was quite pleased by this. He wasn't in the mood for any questions. He quickly brushed his teeth then entered his doorless room. That still pissed him off to no end, but he was just too damn tired to care at this moment. He cast his clothes aside and fell into his soft welcoming bed and within moments he passed out.

He spent the better part of the next week dissecting all that had occurred during his night out with Sydney. While he worked shelving book after book and cleaning up the LCL he constantly had disco songs caught in his head. Thinking of them helped pass the mind-numbingly boring days.

It wasn't until that following Thursday evening that something of note occurred for Albert. After he had eaten yet another spaghetti supper with his mother the phone began to ring. His mother answered while he did the dishes. He stared out the kitchen window at the moon hanging low in the sky and let out a sigh. "Albert, telephone!" Albert quickly turned around. "Albert, a girl wants to speak with you on the phone. She said her name was Olivia." *What the hell...?* Albert thought as he dried his hands upon a crimson hand towel. He grabbed the handset from his mother and took it to his room for some privacy.

"Hello?"

"Hi, Albert! It's Olivia. You know from last weekend?"

"Yeah, I remember."

"Right. I hope I didn't interrupt your dinner or anything."

"Nah, just finished not long ago...How did you get my number?" Albert began to pace back and forth in his room.

"Oh, right! Yeah, I called up Syd and got it."

"...OK. What's up?"

"Yeah, I have a reason why I called! Um, are you planning to come back to the club tomorrow night?"

Albert stopped his pacing for a moment then resumed. "Um, I don't know," Albert said, indecisively.

"Well...I'd like it if you came," Olivia said coyly. Albert stood next to his desk a moment then took a seat.

"I guess I could...I mean I gotta work tomorrow afternoon, but..."

"Oh, where do you work?"

"The LCL."

"Ah, nice. I love that place. It's a nice place to escape from things."

"I used to," Albert said, softly.

"What was that?"

"Nothing. I get off at five. I guess I'll call Syd and tell him to come to pick me up."

"I tell ya what...How about I come and get you this time?"

"You? Well, I wouldn't wanna put you out."

"Nonsense! I called you! It's decided tomorrow at five I'll be there! See ya then."

"Alright then."

"Goodnight, Albert. Looking forward to seeing you again."

"Yeah, sure. Goodnight." And just like that Albert had been roped into another evening at The Sexothèque.

He barely had enough time to process the call when his mother peeped into his room. "Who's Olivia, Alby?"

Albert didn't know exactly how to answer that question. He opted to lie instead of telling the truth. "She's this girl I met at work. She comes into the library for an escape sometimes."

"Ooo, she sounds right up your alley! What did she want?"

*Awfully nosey I must say,* Albert thought. "She invited me out tomorrow night."

"Yeah? On a date?"

"Yeah, I guess."

Albert's mother beamed with happiness. "That's wonderful, Alby!!" She walked over to him and hugged him tightly. I knew you'd meet someone down there eventually! You must invite her over for supper! I want to meet her!"

"Yeah, I'll get right on that."

His mother paid no attention to his sarcastic remark. "I have some more great news for you."

"Oh, rapture. I can't wait to hear this…"

"I knew you would. I've been asked to come back to work…they need me back. They called right before you got home this afternoon. I'll be starting back tomorrow night." Albert stood there a moment. "Isn't that great news?"

"Yeah. That's great."

"I know!! She hugged him tight once more then began to walk out of his room. "Oh, Alby." She looked at his door frame a moment. "I tell you what. Since you might be having Olivia over soon. You'll need your privacy. I'll put your door back up tomorrow while you're at work." She walked over to Albert and looked at him. "Today was a wonderful day," she said then walked back to the living room. He could hear her lightly singing to herself along the way in her usual monotone singing voice. Albert wanted to feel happy for all of this good news, but inside he felt nothing but indifference.

The next day passed along quite like all the rest. Albert's time at work was filled with the usual task of returns and vacuuming the rugs divided between a leftover spaghetti lunch and apprehension on the coming night ahead. Once five o'clock came around Albert clocked out and bid Delores farewell for the weekend. Albert exited the building and found Olivia parked directly out front. So much for bailing. "Albert, hey!" Olivia yelled from the driver's seat. "Hop on in! I got a new mixtape you'll enjoy while we drive over to the club." Albert slunk into the passenger seat and Olivia slid the cassette into the tape deck. He was immediately hit with another smooth base line. He had to admit it was rather catchy.

The music saw him through the night as he sat to the bar nursing another mojito while Olivia talked his ear off. He honestly just sat there listening to the grooves while the world seemed to pass by around him. He was quite content to let it pass him by actually.

The next morning instead of hitting up Denny's they dropped by a different diner. He would have much preferred a Grand Slam breakfast but settled for its equivalent at this little mom and pop place called Danny's. Albert found this a bit funny. It was like some alternate universe Denny's...except not as good.

He threw back a few cups of coffee that tasted like engine oil all the while sitting there as the trio carried on like fools. Albert just sat there tossing around the night's tunes in his head. Pretty soon it was time to go and Sydney ended up dropping Albert off at his home. They said their goodbyes and then Albert made his way inside.

His mother had long since left for work and Albert was greeted to the sound of silence. He quite enjoyed the silence after all of the commotion from the previous night and morning. He looked down the hallway and sure enough his mother had been good on her word. Albert had his door back. "Thank God for that," he said, shattering the silence for a moment. He walked up the hallway and grasped the cool doorknob. It felt pleasant in his warm hand. He turned the knob and opened it. "Ahhh," he sighed. It was such a gratifying feeling to have his door back in place.

This feeling of relief faded rather quickly though when he thought of why she had replaced it. "Fucking ridiculous," he said, walking over to his bathroom. "I know something else that's fucking ridiculous," he said, opening his medicine cabinet and taking out his so-called vitamins. He twisted the cap off and poured every last pill down the toilet. He looked at them float in the bowl for a moment then flushed them down. "Never again," he said, taking the empty bottle. He returned to his room and raised his bedroom window and threw the bottle out into the bushes across from his room. He shut the window and for the first time in a long while he genuinely smiled.

During the next few weeks, Albert could feel a change occur inside of himself. He began to feel as he had before his stint within Duke's End. It began as a slight change where he found himself lost within his daydreams on his breaks at work. He would go outside and sit upon the wooden bench in the reading garden behind the library and before he knew it he would look at his watch and an hour would be lost. Luckily Albert worked relatively fast and stayed out of sight for the most part so no one missed him.

As the days continued to go by he found himself losing gaps of time like this more and more often. He would lose himself completely within his daydreams of Elly. At first, it made him feel elated. He hadn't felt happiness in such a long time. Each time he came out of it though it left him more and more dejected because no matter how long he spent within his thoughts he knew it was all one-sided. Eventually, he found himself simply sitting upon the bench and staring out in the distance at the clouds contemplating, *There must be more to life than this.*

Each day blended seamlessly into the next. Fridays were the only exception to this where Albert would lose himself for the evening within the pulsating disco of The Sexothèque. Olivia continued to grow closer to him but Albert was never really present. Each night he sat upon his stool to the bar and was a million miles away.

During the rest of the days of the week, he was locked in a very specific routine. He found himself waking in the morning, showering, making himself breakfast, and walking to work. After his shift was finished he walked home and saw his mother before she took off again to work her twelve-hour shift at Duke's End.

Since his mother had started working again he hadn't seen too much of her. He didn't mind this at all. The times in which he did see her she would grill him about Olivia and what all they had done on their "dates". Albert came up with details that never happened, which came quite easily since he had spent so many years doing just that in the past. His mother would eat every detail up and smile brightly.

Each time he told her about a fabricated date with Olivia something inside of him would die, but it made his mother ecstatic. He found that after Olivia had come into the picture his mother backed further and further off and threw herself entirely into her work. One evening after he had finished telling her about another made up date his mother had said, "I'm proud of you, Alby. I'm so happy to see that all of this Elly nonsense is over with." She then kissed him upon the crown of his head and departed for another long night at Duke's End. The weight of what she had said hit him immediately and it took everything he had to keep from yelling at her.

Once she was gone Albert screamed at the top of his lungs. "FUCK YOU!" He screamed as he slammed his fists down onto the beige carpet in the living room. As he continued to slam his fists into the floor a thought came to him. *The crawl space...* He needed to check on it. He needed to see if it was still there. He had wanted to check it out for a long time but his mother had been hovering over him for so long since he had returned home he had almost forgotten to look at it.

He jumped to his feet and ran down the hallway into his bedroom. He cast the door open to his closet and knelt. "It has to be here!" He threw some boxes out of the way and found nothing but a plain wall. "No...this can't be! Where the hell is it?!" Albert moved his palms over the wall trying not to panic. He began knocking on the wall trying to see if something might be hidden beneath the wall and sure enough, a place in the back corner produced a hollow sound. He shoved his clothes out of the way and began to kick the spot on the wall.

After one good kick, a portion of the wall broke away revealing a wooden door underneath. He kicked away the rest of the wall around the door frame until it was fully exposed. "How could she do this?! She covered it up! Well, fuck you! It's still here! I'm coming, Elly!!" He placed his hand upon the small doorknob and turned it.

The door remained in place. "What? No, no, no…" He continued to turn the knob and pulled it as hard as he could to no avail. The door remained sealed. He staggered backward. The door stood firmly closed, mocking him. He threw the boxes back into his closet and fell upon the floor beside his bed. He ended up crying himself to sleep upon the floor that night only waking up early that following morning to clean himself up and walk to work.

Later that day while he was mindlessly sorting returns he found himself reflecting upon all of the girls he had ever become infatuated with. When he truly began to dissect each of the times it astounded him. It hit him exactly when all of these infatuations had begun. He had been close to eight years old…it was right after he had gotten back from Duke's End that first time. When he went back to school this girl named Ashley had told him that she had missed him and it made him feel special. After that he found himself falling in love with her…or at least that's how he had always viewed it with every girl that followed.

Looking back at every one of them he could see that he felt nothing but pure infatuation for them. He never loved any of them. He had only felt true love once and not again until Elly came back into his life. He had never stopped to truly think about it but every one of those other girls acted as nothing more than something to fill the void that Elly had left within himself. Coming to this realization didn't offer much solace though, in fact knowing this left Albert feeling even more hopeless than he had before.

Albert decided to leave work early that day and after explaining to Delores that he had a really bad stomach she wished him a quick recovery. He thanked her and set out for his home. While on his walk home he looked up into the bright sky above. Spring was in full force. The late May afternoon sun sat high overhead beating down upon him.

As he walked along he stopped at the crosswalk down the street from the library and stared at the passing traffic as he waited for the light to change. He could vaguely recall some sort of feeling of waiting at a crosswalk once and meeting a girl wearing a baseball cap and sunglasses. He thought he remembered some sort of pin upon her hat, but as quickly as the thought had entered his mind it was gone like vapor in the wind. He shrugged the thought off and continued home.

When he got home Albert tossed his shoes off of his feet and fell upon the couch. He lay there staring up at the ceiling for a few minutes when the phone rang. He grabbed it and looked at the caller ID. It was Olivia. He sighed and pressed the talk button. "Hello?"

"Hey, Albert. I called down to the library looking for you and they said you had left early today. I was worried about you so I figured you must have gone home. You OK, sugar?"

"Oh...yes. I'm fine. I just have a bad stomach. Nothing serious."

"That's good. You want me to come over and look after you?"

"No. That's OK. Um, what were you calling me for earlier?" Albert said, curiously.

"Oh, yeah. I was just gonna call and ask if you were still free tomorrow for supper? You remember we discussed it at Danny's Saturday morning. I think you kind of zoned out there. I wasn't sure if you had heard us or not."

Albert had no recollection of that at all. "Oh, right. Yeah, I remember. I'm still free, yes."

"Oh, good! That's great. How about I pick you up from the library at five tomorrow?" Albert could tell she was smiling when she said this.

"Sounds good...see you tomorrow."

"OK, Albert. I hope you feel better by then."

"I'm sure I will. Goodbye."

"Bye, for now!" He hung up the phone and lied back down upon the couch. He felt completely indifferent about the whole thing.

All he could think about was what his mother had said the day before. *This Elly nonsense is over with...* Those words echoed within his mind. *Tomorrow...what good is tomorrow? All I'm left with now is a future of meaningless tomorrows.* He arose from the couch and made his way to his bedroom where he closed himself within its darkened walls. *I can't go on like this. Like it or not...I've got to see her again...but how?* He lay there for a few minutes pondering this until the darkness claimed him again.

# Chapter 7
# Paradise

Albert arose early the following morning to the smell of sausages frying upon the stove. He turned over and looked at his bedside clock. The clock displayed '7:57'. He wasn't in the mood for breakfast so he turned back over and tried to fall back to sleep for another half hour but a moment later he received a knock upon his door. "Alby? Alby?" He tried to ignore his mother's shrill voice but she wouldn't leave him be.

He hopped out of bed and opened the door. "Yes...?"

"Good morning, Alby. I made some breakfast. I was hoping you and I could catch up a bit before you go off to work. Since I've been working so much here lately I haven't been able to catch you awake."

Albert stared at her a moment. "Sure...I guess so. I'll be out in a minute." She smiled brightly and walked back down the hallway. Albert didn't care to spend any time with his mother, but he felt he needed to keep the charade going. He wanted her to keep believing that everything was going well.

He approached his closet door and looked over his wardrobe. He quickly dressed in a dark purple striped t-shirt and jeans then made haste to the dining room table.

"Good morning. I already made your plate for you." Albert looked at his plate. It was full of breakfast sausages and eggs. A large glass of orange juice sat next to it. He took his seat and began to pick at the eggs.

"So, how has work been going?" Albert asked, staring down into his plate.

"I wanted to talk to you about that. I have some great news. Since I've been working so much here lately and showing initiative they asked if I would be interested in being the head nurse of my unit. I accepted and I'll be starting that position next week!" Albert continued to pick at his eggs. "Isn't that great news, Alby?"

Albert looked up and forced a smile. "That's awesome. You've earned it."

"Thank you, Alby. Well, enough about all that. How are you and Olivia?"

"We're great. I'm going out this evening with her and Syd."

A perplexed look arose upon his mother's face. "Sydney's going to? Is he bringing Victoria?"

"...Um, yeah. Sure," Albert replied.

"Oh, that's cute. A double date."

"Yeah...real cute."

He looked at his watch. '8:35' It read. "Oh, I gotta be going, Ma. I'll see you later."

"Wait, Alby, I'll drop you off today since I'm awake. Come on, let's go!" The two walked outside into the late May morning. Dew cloaked every square inch of their lawn. The sun hit patches and the dew sparkled brilliantly.

"Come on, Alby. Never mind the dew." Albert turned and hopped into the car. As they drove along through the city streets Albert lowered his window and felt the cool early morning air upon his face. It slightly reinvigorated him. "You really must let me meet Olivia. She sounds like a wonderful girl."

"Sure, Ma…" Albert shut his eyes and tried not to think about the day ahead of him.

As usual Albert's day at the library was filled with cart after cart of mundane returns to sort through. He moved at a brisk pace thinking more closely on a topic he had found himself contemplating before he had fallen asleep the night before.

These past few weeks had seen Albert continuously falling further and further into despair. The only thought that seemed to give him any sort of comfort was a thought he had tossed about in his mind ever since coming home from Duke's End. *I have to see Elly again…but how?*

This was a thought he had pondered time and time again. Ever since he came home to find his precious television set thrown out like a mere piece of garbage and discovered the crawl space door sealed shut he had all but given up on the idea of ever being able to be with Elly again…but he couldn't shake the thought that there must be some other way.

As he was tossing about this quandary Delores called out to him."Oh, Albert, I'm sorry to interrupt your sorting but could you do me a favor? Could you run upstairs to the children's room and set up the laserdisc player? I can't make heads nor tails of it."

"Um…sure, Delores. I'll take a look at it."

"Thanks, Albert. You're a peach." *A peach? I wasn't aware I was fuzzy and or pink,* Albert thought as he walked up the staircase to the children's library.

He approached the door and saw a group of about twenty children crowded in front of the library's large television set. Sometimes groups of local school children would take brief field trips here to watch movies and read books. Albert could vaguely remember when he and Sydney came here for a few field trips back in the day. He opened the door and all of the children's gazes fell upon him. They looked at him with wonder. "Are you here to fix the TV, mister?" A young boy asked, curiously.

Albert turned to him and answered. "Yeah. I'll get it all sorted out in no time." The kids gave a unified cheer as Albert approached the TV.

"OK, children. Let's let him work in silence," their teacher said as she sat across from them reading over some school papers from the looks of it. He hit the power button on the TV and it sprung to life. Moments later a bright blue screen faded in. He pressed the power button upon the laserdisc player and it remained lifeless.

Albert looked behind the player and followed the chord. It had come loose from the wall. *Way to go, Delores,* he thought as he rolled his eyes and plugged the player back in. The player sprung to life and Albert walked over to the player and hit eject. The large tray slowly slid out and some of the children were fixated upon it. A children's movie sat upon the player and Albert removed it from the sleeve. Albert slid the huge mirrored disk out of the sleeve and gazed upon it. He noticed the same young boy from before standing next to him staring into it himself.

"You ever wonder if your reflection is yourself in another dimension? Like a backwards world?" the kid said as Albert looked at him through the reflection.

"Can't say I have…do you believe that?"

The kid stood there puzzled for a moment. "Of course, mister."

Albert was intrigued by this young boy's thinking. "So, why do you believe that?"

The young boy didn't miss a beat. "I don't know...I just do. I'm a child. I do not have reasoning for things." With that, the young boy took his seat. Albert placed the movie into the tray and hit play and made his exit, but not without giving one final glance at the young boy in the front row. The boy's total acceptance of something so outlandish without analyzing it in any way reminded him of himself when he was the boy's age.

The rest of the day flew by in a blur for Albert. He mainly stayed in the back corner vacuuming and staring outside at the gathering gloom. Foreboding storm clouds were in the distance and he could tell there was a storm brewing. Five o'clock rolled around not long after and he clocked out and made his way outside. He took a deep breath and opened the door and stepped out into the humid afternoon air. He expected to see Olivia's Jeep parked in her usual spot but it was curiously absent. He looked from left to right and saw no one in sight until a familiar voice called out to him from down the sidewalk. "Yo, Al! Over here!" Sydney yelled out waving his arms.

Albert walked up to him with a look of surprise. "Hey, Syd. I thought Olivia was coming to get me today."

"Yeah, Sharon called me not long ago saying she and Olivia were gonna meet us over there. They're getting all "dolled up", as she put it."

"I see. That's fine. Um, where were we going to eat again?"

"You don't remember, bro? Akane Dragon!"

"Oh, yeah. Now I do."

"I'm gonna have me some steamed clams tonight! I hope you're ready for an unforgettable dinner, Al."

"Yeah…"

As they walked along towards the Miata Sydney looked over at Albert with concern. "You feeling alright, Al? You seem kind of out of it."

Albert looked away from him. "Don't worry about me. Let's just head on over there."

"Alright. Hop in and hold on." Sydney hopped into the driver's seat followed by Albert and they sped off towards Akane Dragon.

Sydney pulled into the parking lot on the side of the building and cruised into a space. Albert had stared vacantly out the window at the city speeding by and didn't notice they had arrived until Sydney killed the engine. "Well, Al, we're here! Damn, I can smell the grub already…You sure you're alright, bro?"

Albert stepped out of the Miata onto the pavement below. "I'm fine…just a bit tired."

"Ah, I hear that. Let's head on inside." Sydney led the way down the narrow sidewalk in front of the building and Albert followed closely behind. A brightly lit neon sign which read, 'BUFFET OPEN ALL YOU CAN EAT' hung in the window of the vestibule inside.

Sydney held the door open for Albert and Albert nodded his head in thanks and stepped into the cool air inside. "Oh, wow. I forgot they had such a bitchin' fountain in here," Sydney said, stepping over and looking into the base of an ornate fountain adorned with an imitation jade dragon encircling the entire fountain. From its mouth, a steady stream of clear water shot back into the collecting pool at the top. "Hey, Al. Remind me to make a wish before we leave, would ya?"

"Yeah, sure," Albert shrugged as he took a seat upon a bright red upholstered chair.

"The ladies should be here soon. Sharon said they'd be here around 5:30." Albert glanced at his watch, '5:25' it read.

Sharon and Olivia finally arrived at 5:45. Albert didn't particularly care about waiting. Sydney paced about back and forth like an expectant father waiting on his child to be born. "There they are! Finally." Sydney held the door open and Sharon came in followed by Olivia. Both were dressed to kill. "Good evening ladies. Glad you could *FINALLY* join us," Sydney said, eyeballing Olivia.

"What are you looking at *ME* for?! Sharon over there is the one who couldn't decide what to wear! She changed like five times!"

"Right…and I'm sure you didn't do the same. Anyway, let's head inside. I want some grub!" Sydney proceeded through the vestibule into the restaurant with Sharon on his arm.

"Hi, Albert. I'm so glad that we could finally have some proper time away from the club."

"Yeah, right. Let's catch up with Syd and Sharon."

"Right. Let's go." Olivia smiled and grabbed onto Albert's arm much as Sharon did with Sydney.

"Table for four, Hiroyuki, my man!" Sydney said to the server that Albert recognized from before. He saw Hiroyuki in here every time he came in wearing his bright yellow collared shirt which read 'Akane Dragon' in dark red letters. Hiroyuki led the four of them to the back portion of the restaurant to a booth beside one of the large circular windows. After taking everyone's drink orders, (Sydney and Sharon ordered a bottle of saké and Albert and Olivia both ordered Pepsi), he left them to help themselves to the buffet. "You guys ready? Let's head on up," Sydney said, letting Sharon walk ahead of him. Albert followed behind everyone. His gaze fixed upon the floor mostly.

As everyone loaded up their plates Albert looked at the spread staring back at him. He quickly threw some chicken fried rice and noodles upon his plate along with some fried bite-sized shrimp. "Yo, check it out, Al," Sydney said, showing off his tightly stacked plate of food. The steamed clams he mentioned he was going to eat sat proudly atop the mound of food. "Ahh, yeah!" Sydney smiled as he walked back to the table. Albert looked down at his plate and decided he had enough for now and he returned to the table himself.

The table erupted with the sounds of talking and laughter from everyone but Albert. Olivia turned to Albert and told him she had a surprise for him. Albert slowly turned towards her and saw that she had a cassette in her hands. "This is for you. I got D.B. to record a full mixtape for you of all the songs in his setlist this past weekend." Albert slowly took the cassette and read the white label on Side A. It read, 'TO ALBERT - TIMELESS DISCO'. He flipped the tape over and saw Side B read, 'XO OLIVIA'.

"Thank you very much, Olivia. I'll treasure it," he said, sliding the cassette into his pocket.

"Oh, lord…did she really give you a cassette of that crap? Do me a favor, Al. Let me know when you're gonna play it so I'm not around," Sydney said, throwing back a shot of saké and then pouring another from the clear teal-colored bottle that Hiroyuki had left at the table.

"Yo, Syd! Don't talk shit about disco! How many times do I gotta tell ya!" Olivia said as she threw a bite-sized shrimp across the table hitting Sydney on his forehead. This caught Sydney by surprise and made him as well as the rest of the table, (minus Albert), erupt into laughter.

Olivia began telling Albert about what all she had been up to that afternoon with getting ready and Albert sat staring out the window tuning her out. "What do you think of my outfit, Albert?" she asked as he picked at his chicken fried rice.

"Very lovely," he replied. She wrapped her arm around him and thanked him. She was genuinely happy. Albert could see that. He turned away from her and continued staring out the window. He began to watch the cars passing by on the street and saw his reflection staring back at him.

Another neon sign flickers into life across the street beyond his reflection and he adjusted his eyes upon it. 'Mick's Pawn' the bright yellow sign read. Besides the neon sign within the pawnshops display window sat something which made Albert's eyes widen. A faux wood-paneled television set sat upon an oak table. It was a television much like the one he had had but slightly different. *Dear God...that's it!! I know what I must do!!* The thought screamed inside of him so loudly that for a moment he wasn't sure if he had yelled it out.

"Yo, Syd, can I borrow your keys real quick? I forgot my wallet in the car." Everyone turned and looked at Albert for a moment.

"Sure, thing, bro. Here you go." He laid the keys out on the table and Albert scooped them up.

"...Can I get out real quick, Olivia?"

"Oh, sure, Albert. I gotta hit the ladies' room anyway." Olivia slid out of the booth followed by Albert. Albert turned for a moment and looked at Sydney.

"Yeah, bro?"

"Nothing...thanks, Sydney." Albert turned away and walked towards the entrance. Once he made it outside he prayed that Sydney and Sharon wouldn't notice that he didn't walk past the window towards the car. He thanked God for the small blessing that Olivia had decided to go to the restroom. He made his way to the curb and looked both ways before sprinting across the street towards Mick's and the brightly glowing neon sign that beckoned to him.

Upon entering Mick's, a loud cowbell tied to the door announced his presence. An old man reading a newspaper behind a glass display counter full of handguns looked up and locked eyes with Albert. "Good afternoon, son. What can I do ya fer?" the old man said, putting the paper down upon the countertop.

Albert slowly approached the counter looking around at the eclectic collection of items for sale. He could see musical instruments tucked into the back portion of the store. Complete drum sets, expensive-looking keyboards, and electric guitars sat waiting to be played by anyone willing to pay the price tag. Shelves of VHS tapes lie before the instruments. Albert could spot VCRs and even a few laserdisc players.

"Hello, sir. I was wondering if I could purchase that television from your display window there."

"You wanna buy THAT?" the old man said, looking at Albert over the rim of his wire frame glasses.

"Yes, sir. How much is it?"

"Not for sale, son."

Albert furrowed his brow. "I'll pay you good money for it. Name your price."

The old man turned away from Albert and picked his paper up. "Sorry, son, that ain't gon' work. Besides the damn thing's busted. Why would you wanna go and buy a busted TV?"

"I don't care that it's busted. I need it. Now name your price, old man."

The old man laid his paper down once more and with a smug grin upon his face looked at Albert. "Son, the name's Mick. Not "old man"…if you really want the old girl I guess I could let her go fer…" He trailed off and then held up two fingers.

"Twenty dollars? Fine. You got it."

Mick shook his head. "Guess again, son."

"OK…two hundred? That's fine."

"Nope."

Albert, clearly upset, slammed his hands down upon the counter. "Out with it then, Mick. What do you want?"

"Two thousand. Take it or leave it."

"What kind of place are you running here? Two grand for an outdated busted television set! You must be joking!"

"Oh, I'm as serious as a heart attack. Ole Mick don't mess around. I've grown quite attached to that set. That's why she's in the window there. Seems to me you want that set pretty bad and what with supply and demand I can give it any price I want." Mick burst out in a fit of laughter with his mouth so wide Albert could see he only had a handful of teeth left. "Is there anything else I can do fer ya, son? How about one of the other sets in the back there?"

Albert turned and looked at some bulky cabinet-sized television sets he imagined were from the 70s if not earlier. "No thanks. They...aren't what I'm looking for."

"OK, son. Don't..." Just as Mick was about to tell Albert don't let the door hit ya where the good lord split ya a phone began to ring from the back office. "Ah, hell...excuse me a sec. Why don't you think about my offer a bit, son," Mick said, bursting into another fit of laughter.

Mick stepped into the back office and Albert could hear him chatting away on the phone. He began looking around the shop. His eyes fixated upon the door to the display window. He could see no cameras set up anywhere. He imagined that if Mick still had a cowbell on the door he might not have any security cameras installed.

He stepped around behind the display counter and walked over to the door and opened it up. Inside the display window, the television set looked even more enticing up close. *Two thousand dollars...I can't pay that. That greedy old bastard has another thing coming,* Albert thought as he stepped into the window display. Through the window, he looked across the street for a moment and could see Sydney and Sharon chatting away completely unfazed by his absence. It appeared that Olivia was still in the restroom. "Thank God," Albert muttered as he swooped in and grabbed the television set up from the table. It was a little heavy but he clutched the precious cargo safely within his arms.

He closed the display door behind him and something else caught his eye within the shop. He placed the set upon the glass counter and opened the display and pulled out a silver revolver with a wooden grip and a box of bullets. Albert stared at the gun for a moment. *I'm gonna be seeing Elly one way or another,* he thought solemnly. He began to load the revolver when he heard Mick wrapping up his call. He managed to load three bullets into the chambers and tucked it into the waist of his jeans. He quickly grabbed the television set and slammed through the door back onto the street outside.

As soon as he set foot back onto the street a strong gust of wind hit him nearly toppling him over. He regained his balance and looked around at the various trees planted along the sidewalk and how their branches swayed wildly. He looked into the sky and saw the storm clouds which were in the distance an hour or so before had finally descended upon Lando. A flash of lightning lit up the street for a moment which a few seconds later was followed by a low rumble of thunder.

*I don't have much time...* he thought as he took off running down the sidewalk. He could see the Miata parked along the side of Akane Dragon now and he sprinted across the street. He quickly ran to the passenger side of the car and realized the top was down. *Thank God Sydney was out of it and didn't realize that I didn't need the keys...*

He opened the passenger door and laid the television set upon the seat. He placed his hand upon it for a moment thinking back to what the kid at the library said, I'm a child. I do not have reasoning for things. That's the mindset Albert had needed this entire time. Just because he didn't have the TV Syd had given him didn't mean that it was all over. No, not at all. The TV never had the power itself. He did. It was inside of himself all along. He just let the reasoning of an adult mind stand in his way. This wasn't meant to be over thought. You just went with it.

He closed the passenger door and a soft voice came from behind him. "Albert? What's going on?"

He quickly turned around to find Olivia standing there behind him. "Olivia...I..."He started but trailed off not knowing how to explain himself.

"I saw you running down the street for dear life holding onto something." She looked over at the TV sat upon the passenger seat. "Why do you have an old TV, Albert? What's going on? Talk to me!"

Albert stood there a moment overwhelmed. "I...I need it, Olivia. I'm sorry, but I haven't the time to explain all of this to you. I need to go." He walked over to the driver's door but Olivia slammed it shut when he tried to open it.

"No! Talk to me, Albert. I can help you. I know I tend to talk a lot and I haven't let you get a lot in edgewise, but I want to know what's going on. You always seem so distant. Is this about Elly? You can talk to me about her..."

Albert had been staring down at the pavement, but when Olivia mentioned Elly he looked up at her into her eyes. "Where did you hear that name?"

"Syd told me...he didn't say much. Just that you cared about her a lot and that she wasn't around anymore. I'm sorry that she's gone, Albert. Truly I am. I...dealt with similar circumstances a few years ago when my boyfriend passed."

"I never said anything about her being dead. I said she was gone to a place where we can't meet again....That's all going to change today though. Now let me get into the car."

Tears began to stream down Olivia's face. "I don't understand, Albert, but I don't want you to leave...I love you. I can be here for you right now." She wrapped her arms around his waist and then stopped and lifted his shirt. "Albert, what the hell is this?!" Olivia stared horrified at the wooden grip of the revolver sticking out of Albert's pants.

"Olivia...please! I have to go." He shoved Olivia aside and entered the Miata.

"Albert, what are you planning?! Are you going to kill yourself? We can talk about this! Let me help you."

Albert looked into her dark eyes for a moment and spoke. "Nobody can help me, Olivia. If I can't be with Elly...then there's just no point in going on. There's only one thing left for me to do. The only thing I can do to be truly happy again."

He started the car and looked back at her as he shifted into drive. "Olivia...another time and place we could have been great. ...Do me one final favor, please. Tell Sydney I'm sorry. I always thought of him as a brother," he said, removing his foot from the brake and speeding off.

As he turned onto the street he looked into the rearview mirror and saw Olivia standing there on the curb watching as he drove away. As he passed by the window he glanced over and he thought he caught a brief glimpse of Sydney looking out at him. He sped through the city streets as the wind blew through his hair and dried the tears that had fallen down his cheeks. He looked over at the television set rocking back and forth upon the seat and put his hand upon it. "I'm coming, Elly. Wait for me just a little longer."

Albert sped through the winding streets of Lando praying that a police car wouldn't appear out of anywhere to come to haul him away for stealing not only a TV but a revolver. Even worse he prayed that a car from Duke's End wouldn't come for him with Mort behind the wheel with those huge hands of his ready to pluck Albert up and never let him see the light of day again. He shook these thoughts from his mind and continued to drive.

A few minutes later he pulled into his driveway and killed the engine. The sky above looked black and menacing. A huge bolt of lightning forked across the sky above and was immediately followed by a deafening boom of thunder. He could feel small drops of rain beginning to fall upon his face. He ran to the passenger side door and reached inside and grabbed the TV and immediately ran into the house before it could get any worse.

He slammed the door behind him and was greeted by the usual silence and darkness of his empty home. He wasted no time in running up the hall to his room. Surely Olivia had informed Sydney of him taking off with his car as well as the TV and even worse the gun. He expected he wouldn't have long before someone showed up here looking for him. Maybe he should have parked the Miata further up the street? No, with that storm about to unleash outside he was lucky to have beaten it here.

He placed the TV upon his reading desk exactly where the previous one had sat. He unraveled the power cord and plugged it into the wall and then pulled the power knob out...nothing. Sure, enough. That old bastard was right. The TV it seemed was busted...but that hadn't stopped the other one from serving its purpose. *OK, think! How can I get Elly's attention? How can I let her know I'm here?!* Albert stood staring at the TV for what felt like ages when another clap of thunder overhead shook the entire house. Albert could feel the thunder shake him to his very core. He thought about this a moment and realized what he needed to do next. From within himself, he needed to call out to Elly.

A moment later from behind him Albert heard the front door open. "Alby?!" Surprise. Surprise. It was his mother. *Sweet Jesus! She didn't waste any time!* Albert thought as he flung his door shut, firmly locking it. "ALBY! Open this door right now! Sydney called me and told me about everything! You're not well...please, let me in! We can take care of this!"

Albert turned towards his door and angrily yelled, "Yeah, right! All you wanna do is lock me up in that godforsaken loony bin again! Never again!! I'm going to see Elly, and there's not a damn thing you can do to stop me this time!"

A moment passed and Albert thought maybe she had left, but loud bangs came upon his door. "ELLY DOES NOT EXIST, ALBERT!! WHY CAN'T YOU LET HER GO?!"

"I haven't the time to waste talking about this with you. You'll never understand," Albert said as calmly as he could. He could hear her running up the hallway a moment later.

Finally, a moment of calm followed. Albert didn't know where his mother had gone and he didn't care. Within this moment Albert collected his thoughts and began to concentrate. *Elly? Are you there, Elly? I need you. Please, come to me.* He began to think this phrase over and over until he was in an almost trance-like state. WHAM WHAM WHAM His eyes flew open and he looked at his door.

"I'm coming, Albert! I'm coming! I won't let you hurt yourself!" his mother screamed as she continued to try and knock his door down. It appeared his mother was attempting to knock his door handle off and destroy the lock.

"Like hell, you will," Albert said to himself as he stepped beside his large shelf packed full of countless books. He threw his entire body against the side of it and screamed out as he tipped it over blocking the door frame.

A moment later his mother knocked the door handle off and pushed the door open only to find it wasn't budging. "Damn it, Albert! I'm not giving up! I'll be back!" She yelled as she ran down the hallway.

*Damn it! Elly, I need you! Please!* he thought as he eyeballed his window. He didn't know how this was going to play out. He had hoped he would be long gone by now but Elly was still nowhere to be found. He raised his window open and a gust of wind immediately hit his face splashing raindrops upon the lenses of his glasses. He took the revolver out and laid it upon the window sill. He took a deep breath and for a moment he contemplated making a run for it. It was only a matter of time before his mother was going to get in and she'd be followed by God only knew who else. He set one foot upon the sill and was just about to jump out when he turned around and looked at the television set. It sat there as it had within Mick's display window beckoning him. He stepped down from the sill and decided to gather his thoughts one final time. He tuned everything else out. The raging storm outside and the one inside banging upon his door frame again. He closed his eyes, cleared his mind, and thought of Elly's face. He thought of calling out to her as he had tried that last time from the "window frame". He thought of her standing beneath the three palms as the storm was about to roll in off of the bay. *Elly...Elly! ELLY! I NEED YOU! PLEASE, COME TO ME! I LOVE YOU!* Every fiber of his being screamed out.

He could feel something from deep within himself begin to awaken. It was a nostalgic feeling he hadn't felt in a long time. "Love?" Albert opened his eyes to find the television screen sprung to life. Upon the screen standing upon the platinum sand of their beach stood Elly. The wind lightly blew her fiery bangs.

"Elly?! Oh, my God! It's you! I can't believe it!" Tears began to fill Albert's eyes.

"Yes, Love! I heard you calling out to me. I haven't been able to reach you for a long time. What happened?"

"I know, Elly. SO much has happened! I've been waiting for you for so long. I never thought I'd see you again. I'm so sorry to have kept you waiting!"

Elly began to cry herself. "Oh, Albert. I was never going anywhere. I'd have waited for you forever."

"ALBY?! Who are you talking to in there? What are you doing?!" Albert's mother began to yell from the hallway as she continued to chip away at the door frame stopping her from entering the room.

"Love, what is going on over there?!" Albert threw a glance over his shoulder at his door frame. She had already chipped away a quarter of it.

"It's a long story…I'll tell you about it soon. I need to get out of here."

Elly looked behind Albert and saw what was happening. "Yes, it certainly is high time that this happens. Before I bring you though I need to tell you something. Something I was going to tell you Valentine's night or rather show you. It's something you still haven't remembered from the past that you need to know."

Albert stood in front of Elly as she began to lift the final piece of the veil from within Albert's mind. As he stood there he felt his mind drifting back…far back to a time he'd long since forgotten.

"Alright, boys. I'm going out to pick up some groceries. You want anything, love?" Albert's mother spoke.

"Nah, I'm good. What about you, Alligator?!"

"I'm good, daddy-o."

"Daddy-o?! Come here, you." Albert began to run around jumping on the furniture trying to get away from his father.

"Oh, you guys. Try not to destroy the house while I'm out." Albert's mother grabbed her purse and walked outside. Before she shut the door she looked back at the two of them laughing so loudly and little Al with a great big smile upon his face.

"Well, since your mother is going to be gone awhile I wanna share something with you."

"What is it?" Little Al asked curiously.

"Come on, Alligator! I wanna show you something!" He followed his father to his parent's bedroom where his father plucked something out of their closet. Little Al could feel the excitement building inside of him. They then returned to the living room where his father took a seat upon the couch. Al could feel the beige carpet beneath his small toes and jumped into his father's arms upon the couch.

"Whoa, slow it down there."

"What are we gonna look at, Daddy?" Al's father grabbed the remote sitting upon the coffee table.

"I'm going to show you paradise, Al."

Al's eyes grew wide with wonder. "What's that?" Al asked.

"Ho, ho! You'll see, my son."

His father pressed a button and the screen flashed on. Upon the screen, little Al watched as a beach came into view from a balcony window. He could hear the laughter of his mother and father in the background.

The scene jumped then to a shot of the sun hanging low in the sky above a bay of shimmering, crystal clear water. The camera panned out revealing platinum white sands and a woman sat upon a wooden beach chair. The camera drew closer to her as she turned around smiling ear to ear. It was his mother. She looked so young and beautiful sitting there. Her normally long hair was cut short with long bangs.

"That's Ma?"

"Yeah, Al. Pretty wasn't she? She still is I gotta say. She's just as lovely as the day I married her."

Little Al's eyes grew even wider. "Where is paradise, Daddy?"

"This was filmed during our honeymoon when we went to the Caribbean. The name of the place is The Isle of Elise."

"Wow..." Al continued to watch the screen as it panned over the tropical scenery.

"Can you keep a secret, Al?"

"Of course!" Al said, enthusiastically.

"I'm taking your mom back there soon for Valentine's Day...and you're coming too."

"WHAT?! I get to see paradise?!"

"Yes, Alligator!" Little Al could hardly contain himself. "Now, son, I need you to promise me you'll not breathe a word of this to your mother. It's going to be a surprise. Do you understand?"

Al shook his head up and down. "OK, daddy-o!"

"That's my boy!" his father said, giving him a big hug. "OK, Alligator, I'm gonna make us some hot cocoa. Do you want marshmallows in yours?"

"Yes, please!" Al turned back to the television screen and was sad to see that the video had finished. "Daddy, can I watch it again?"

"Sure thing, Al. Just hit rewind and then play when it stops."

"Got it." "Al said, scanning over the buttons. He located the rewind button and pressed it. He could see everything going in reverse. "Whoa, neat," he said, sitting on the couch captivated by every frame.

A few minutes later Albert's father returned. "OK, my boy. Let's watch this again." The tape finished rewinding and began to automatically play. His father sat next to Albert and put his arm around him. Little Al must have sat there watching the tape for a good hour before he realized his father never got the hot cocoa.

"Hey, Daddy, you forgot the cocoa." He looked up at his father who appeared to be fast asleep. "Daddy? OK...we'll forget the cocoa then." He continued to watch the video until his mother came home that evening.

"Hi, boys. Don't help me or anything. It's fine."

"Shh. Sorry, Ma. Daddy's asleep."

"Asleep?" his mother said, shocked. "Well, it's time for Daddy-o to wake up." She walked over to him and shook his shoulder. "Come on, love. Time to get up." He continued to sit there. "Don? Come on. Wake up."

She shook him harder this time and Al stood up and shook him too. His father fell forward off of the couch and landed face first upon the carpet. Albert's mother screamed and immediately picked up the phone and dialed 911.

Little Al knelt next to his father and continued to shake him. "Daddy? Why aren't you waking up?" His mother placed her hand upon his shoulder and told Al to go play in his room. Al obeyed but looked over once more at his mother shaking his father. "Please, wake up, love."

Al sat in his room in the darkness as he heard his mother go outside then come back in followed by the voices of several men. He heard them all talking to his mother as they discussed his father. Then his mother began sobbing loudly. She let out a sound that Albert had never heard from her before. It was a sound of pure sorrow. He couldn't take hearing it.

He ran into his closet and closed the door behind him. As he sat in silence he thought of that island and how things were perfect there. "Paradise" his father had called it. *What was the name of the island again? El something...* he thought. He began to imagine himself there on that beach. He could still hear his mother's cries cutting through every few minutes. He clamped his hands together and prayed that something could help him. *I wish everything was alright!* he thought as he sat in the darkness.

Everything went quiet then and a voice began to speak to him. It was the soft voice of a girl. She spoke with an accent that Albert's father had. His father had once told Albert that he came from a faraway land called England. Little Al knew nothing of England but he loved the way his father spoke.

*I'm here, love. Don't worry. Everything's gonna be alright.* Al didn't believe he had heard anything at first. *Are you there, love? You can speak to me. Even with your mouth closed. Use your mind.*

*What's your name? Where are you?* Albert spoke but not from his mouth but within his mind.

The voice began to giggle. *That's good, love. I don't have a name. As for where I am. It's total darkness here, but that's OK because I feel you. I know you're there and that makes me happy.*

Albert spent hours talking to the voice. It completely drowned out everything else. Before he knew it his eyes began to grow heavy. *You rest, love. I'll be here tomorrow. Just call out when you need me and I'll be there. Goodnight, Albert.*

The following days were a whirlwind for Little Al. He found himself being watched after by his aunt Lolita and uncle Harry for many of them. He enjoyed spending time with Sydney though. The two of them played his Atari a lot and Al found this offered a nice distraction for himself. He tried to talk to Sydney about the video his father had shown him but Sydney showed no interest in hearing about "some boring island" as he had put it. This disappointed Al, but the voice spoke to him saying, *Don't worry about Sydney. He'll understand one day.* Al took comfort in this.

The following day saw Albert going to a large cold brick building where station wagon looking cars parked lined up on the side. Al didn't like this place. It radiated sadness. He needed the voice now more than ever. He shut out everything around him and the voice offered him a warm blanket of blindness as well as deafness. A thick veil as it were which nothing penetrated. Al coasted through those dark days not truly seeing anything. He couldn't bare to see or hear any of it. His father would always live within his heart...not within some shiny ornate casket. There were only two words Al had caught said by his uncle Harry while he and Sydney had been playing the Atari. "Brain aneurysm." Al knew what the first word meant but as for the second word he had no idea.

Months passed by and Al saw himself growing ever closer to the voice. When he returned to school, shortly after everything had settled down, his classmates didn't know what to say to him which caused Al to delve further within himself. Each day Al became more and more closed off until his mother began to become concerned. "Alby? Your teachers say you barely speak in class anymore. Talk to me. What's on your mind?"

Little Al stood there a moment with a puzzled look upon his face. "I talk all day, Ma. Just not out loud."

"Who are you talking to?"

"To the voice of the girl inside my head."

His mother began to look at Al very concerned. "What's her name?"

"She doesn't have one."

The following weekend, after he and his mother's conversation, saw Al lying in bed late Friday night. He was talking to the voice as usual when he asked her a question. *When can I see you?*

A moment passed. *How about tonight, love? I'll get everything ready for you. You take a nap and I'll see you soon.*

*OK! I can't wait!* little Al replied as he rolled over and tried to sleep. He tossed and turned and lay there in bed for what felt like eons. He was about to call out to her again when a flash of light came from his closet.

Perplexed by this he hopped out of bed and opened his closet door. The light permeated the cracks of the small door which lead to the crawl space. His parents told him never to go playing around in there and he obeyed but the bright light was like a siren song to him and he just couldn't ignore it.

He opened the small door and the light quickly faded away. He knelt and looked through the door and could smell a damp scent. It was the smell of a cave. Al could make out a bright light at the end of this cave. He crawled upon his hands and feet entering the doorway. Upon entering the cave he could feel the damp earth beneath him. He pressed onward finding that the cave widened as it went along and he could stand up. As he stood he broke into a jog wanting to reach the light at the end. As he drew closer he could swear he heard the sounds of many tropical birds squawking in the trees ahead.

He reached the light and it was full of warmth. Al had missed the feeling of the sun on his skin. He stood there a moment letting it sink in when he began to hear the sound of waves upon the wind. He began to beat his way through the thicket ahead of him. The further forward he went the sound of the waves grew louder.

Al found himself finally pressing through the thicket and stepping out onto the platinum white dunes of a beach never set upon by anyone before. The pure unspoiled splendor was an amazing sight to behold. He took his first step upon the virgin sand and walked towards the crystal clear glistening water.

Within the water, Al looked down and could see hundreds of small tropical fish of all the colors in the rainbow. He heard splashing further out in the water and looked up. He saw two neon pink dolphins jumping up out of the water. He watched them a moment and then they came swimming close to the shore. Al trekked out into the warm water where they stayed waiting for him. Their skin appeared to be coated in an immeasurable amount of sparkles. He rubbed his hands over their smooth faces and they both squealed happily at him then swam back into the deeper waters of the bay.

He made his way back onto the beach, where the waves crashed upon his feet, and stood there a moment in utter disbelief. As he stood there he felt someone tap him upon his shoulder and he fell forward in shock.

He picked himself up off the sand and turned around to find a young girl giggling. The sun shined down upon her and caused her vibrant fiery red hair to appear alive. Her hair fell past her shoulders and her long bangs slightly hid her left eye. "Hello, love," she said, extending her arm to him. He grabbed her hand and noticed how soft it was.

"So, this is where you've been this whole time."

"Well..." She began then looked around. "It didn't always look like this. Remember when I said there used to be nothing but darkness? Each day after that a new feature would present itself. The sea, the sky, the land..."

"All of this just came together?" he said, amazed.

"Yes, love. I was the last thing to be given a form. I woke up with you one day and found I had hands and feet. An entire body just appeared overnight."

"Wow, bitchin'," Al said. "Sorry, Syd said that a while back and I was shocked. We're not supposed to curse."

She began to laugh at this. "You can say whatever you want here, Albert. No one's around but the two of us!"

Albert looked around and drew in a breath and yelled out, "BITCHIN'!!" The two of them let out a fit of laughter at his outburst.

"So, now that you have a body. Do you have a name?"

She looked down at her feet. "No. I still don't have one of those."

"Well, that's no good. Today I'm gonna change that," he said and began to contemplate a name for her. He thought of his father and the paradise he had shown him. *I've got it!*

He told her to kneel then placed his hand upon her shoulder. "From this day forward you will be known as Elly and this place...The Isle of Elly." Elly rose to her feet. "How does it feel to have a name, Elly?"

"I love it!" she said, hugging Albert tightly and kissing him upon his cheek. Albert turned a shade redder than Elly's hair.

Albert found himself spending the rest of the day with Elly upon the beach and when the night came she showed him to a small house by the sea. It had been where Elly had woken up with her body. When he entered the place he immediately felt at home. He stayed there talking with Elly and looking out upon the moonlit bay until he couldn't keep his eyes open anymore. At that time Elly led him back to the cave.

"I'm going to miss you," she said.

"I'll miss you too. We'll still talk though as we always have and don't worry I'll be back tomorrow! I mean if you want..."

Elly laughed, "Of course I do, Albert! You can come back tomorrow night after bedtime."

"OK! See ya then, Elly!" he said and waved goodbye then crawled back through the damp cave. The next day came and Albert spent the entire day "talking" to Elly. She loved it when he called her by her new name. It made her feel incredibly happy. Al and his mother went out for lunch together but he spent the entirety of it speaking to Elly. His mother became increasingly concerned as the days rolled by.

As the days turned into weeks Albert began visiting Elly more and more frequently and found it harder to leave. Pretty soon he ended up spending entire days upon the Isle of Elly only coming home in small, infrequent bursts throughout.

As he began spending more time there he noticed something. Each time he visited their home by the sea it would be slightly larger from the time before as if to reflect the place within himself that Elly continued to build each time he saw her.

He began to feel a need to see her every day. Talking to her was all well and good but nothing could replace the feeling he got of wrapping his arms around her and feeling the warmth emanate from her. He began to make excuses to stay in his room and not to be disturbed. Then came the day where he didn't come home at all.

Albert remembered all too well where that lead. It led down the hardest, loneliest road he had ever been down. Thankfully though that road was ending directly ahead.

Albert came back to the present. The veil had finally been fully removed. He'd seen the truth and looked into Elly's eyes. *My God...I forgot. How could I forget?* He spoke but not out loud. *I've known you since that day...you came to me when I called out into the void.*

*I was born that day, love. I was born...to love you.* Tears fell from both of their faces. Behind Albert, his mother had nearly broken into his room. She was but a mere quarter away from taking the door frame off with her sledgehammer. *Now's the time, love. I want you to touch the screen and take my hands.*

*This was what you had planned back in February?*

*Yes, love. I spent years coming to you in your dreams, but you can't get to me from your dreams. You need a more concrete portal than that. Something you can latch an idea onto. You see the crawl space door worked because you read once in a book about entering another world through such a doorway.*

*And the television set?*

*Yes, that...do you remember that one film you and Syd rented when you were in high school that he hated and you disliked too but the premise stayed with you. There was something about it you couldn't shake about entering another world through a TV.* Albert understood it. He didn't dissect it. That kid's words echoed in his mind again briefly when he heard another piece of his door frame go flying off. *Come, love. We haven't much time left.*

*Wait...* Albert thought as he turned around quickly and ran over to his closet door. He swung the door open and delved into his bag and pulled out his old sketchbook. *Now! I didn't want to leave without this!* He slid it into his back pocket and Elly smiled at him.

*OK, love. It's time. Now touch the screen.*

Albert looked at the screen, it looked crystal clear much as it had before. It was too clear for a television set...especially one from the 1980s! He pressed his hands upon the screen and to his shock, they went through! He could see his hands within the screen itself and pressed further, deeper still.

His fingers, then his hands, arms were totally within the screen. "That's good, love. Now take my hands." He grabbed her hands and he remembered just how soft they had been. He pressed his head into the screen and closed his eyes tightly.

Sound became distorted for a moment. The loud banging behind him became muffled as he pressed deeper. "That's it, love! You're almost there!" He could feel himself becoming elevated as if he were floating. He held his eyes firmly shut but could feel himself sinking ever deeper. He could hear the sound of ocean waves crashing against the beach and Elly grunting as she pulled him in.

The final blow came down upon the door frame and Albert's mother swung the door aside. She stood for a moment in utter disbelief at the sight of Albert's legs dangling in mid-air as they slowly crept further into the TV. She came to her senses and made a leap over the fallen bookshelf in front of her and went to grab for one of his legs. She came up short and landed on her face upon the carpet hitting her head hard upon the adjacent wall.

She quickly shook off the fall and reached up to grab for his feet but it was too late. She stood up to see Albert on the screen lying upon the platinum white sand with his hands being held by a woman with short fiery red hair. She helped him to his feet and they both embraced one another tightly. Albert's mother stood watching in utter amazement. A moment later Albert turned to face his mother. "Hi, Ma. There's someone I've been wanting to introduce to you for a very long time. You always wanted to be the first person to meet my girlfriend. Well, this is Elly."

"Hi, there," Elly managed to say. She could tell that Albert's mother wasn't too pleased to meet her.

"Albert? What's going on? Where are you?"

"I'm on the Isle of Elly now, Ma. The place I've always talked about, but no one believed existed. Look around! It's just as real as you or me or Elly herself!"

Albert's mother turned away from the screen. "No. This can't be real. Where are you?!"

"I told you, Ma. I'm here with Elly…and I'm never coming back. You drove me to this. You could have been here too if you hadn't decided to toss me into that damned Duke's End like some kind of lunatic!"

"Never coming back?! WHAT?!"

"You heard me. I'm living the rest of my days here with Elly. I'd dream of being nowhere else." Albert grabbed Elly's hand and began to walk away from the screen.

"WAIT!" his mother screamed.

Albert turned back one more time. "I need to be going. I hate goodbyes. I'll always remember you, Ma. I'm sorry that it had to come to this. I never wanted it to be this way. I just want you to know that."

Albert continued to walk along the beach when Elly cast a look over her shoulder. Albert's mother internalized it as Elly saying 'You lose bitch.' She began to bang upon the television. Hitting the sides slightly distorting the picture.

"You bitch! How dare you!" she screamed out. She looked over at the open window where the revolver still sat upon the sill. She grabbed it, cocked the gun, aimed right at Elly, and fired. With a loud bang, the television screen erupts in a bright flash of light and smoke. When the smoke settled she gazed into the exploded screen of the TV and sat there unable to move.

Albert never looked back at the loud explosion behind them. He kept walking down the platinum white sands holding onto Elly's hand. He looked over at her with tears in his eyes. "I'm sorry, love. I wish things could have been different with her too. It never should have come to this," she said, throwing her arms around him. He closed his eyes and buried his face into her hair. She smelled just as she had in his dreams.

He continued holding her a moment longer and whispered into her ear, "I love you, Elly."

"I love you too, Albert," she whispered back. As they continued down the beach a large palatial estate rose into view. "It sure has gotten bigger since the last time I was here," Albert said.

"Yes, love. The design is so seamless though you'd never be able to tell from the original architecture."

"I can't wait to see it."

"There's someone there that wants to see you. He's missed his daddy."

"...Tony. We'll have to take him out for a day on the beach. I've missed my boy. I hope he's been as good as gold." Elly smiled brightly and shook her head.

As they continued onward past their home by the sea Albert could make out three familiar trees in the distance. "The three palms..." They swayed back and forth in the light breeze coming off of the bay. Albert looked around at the paradise surrounding him and then back at Elly.

She looked into his eyes a moment then yelled, "Race you to the trees!" She took off and for a moment Albert gazed upon her as she ran down the beach. His eyes fell upon her mouth and that adorable little mole next to it and watched as a wide smile formed upon her beautiful face. He had never felt such happiness in his entire life.

He took off after her and caught up but let her win as he had done all those years before. "You slowpoke. Some things never change," she said, laughing. Albert took her in his arms and pulled her close. He kissed her deeply as they stood there beneath the three palms.

As Albert held Elly close to him the two watched in silence as the sun slowly set on this day. Elly rested her head upon his shoulder and he squeezed her tightly. He knew that he'd finally found his happiness and that he'd never let her go again.

January 1, 2019 - October 30, 2019
Childersburg, Alabama

# About Dino Jones

Dino Jones's Motto:
"I like to jerk those tears.
When I come up with ideas I tend to lean more toward the emotional melancholic side. I find stories like that to be quite interesting. If I can stir emotion within the reader and even jerk a few tears out I feel like I've accomplished my goal and then some."

Within, his debut novel, 'Born From A Wish', Mr. Jones delves into themes of loneliness and trying to find one's place in this world...even if it's within your own little world.

Dino Jones was born and raised in Sylacauga, Alabama. He's lived in Alabama for most of his life but also lived in Newfoundland, Canada, and Laredo, Texas.

Mr. Jones has a lot of stories kicking around in his mind and is quite eager to share them. Stick around because some things last a long time…

Printed in Great Britain
by Amazon